ANNIE'S RAINBOW

ANNIE'S RAINBOW

Fern Michaels

severn
House

This title first published in Great Britain 1999 by
SEVERN HOUSE PUBLISHERS LTD of
9–15 High Street, Sutton, Surrey SM1 1DF.
First published in the USA 2000 by
SEVERN HOUSE PUBLISHERS INC., of
595 Madison Avenue, New York, NY 10022,
by arrangemnt with Kensington Publishing Corporation.

British Library Cataloguing in Publication Data

Michaels, Fern
          Annie's rainbow
          1.   Love stories
          I.   Title
          813.5'4 [F]

          ISBN 0-7278-5477-1

Printed and bound in Great Britain by
MPG Books Ltd, Bodmin, Cornwall.

CHAPTER ONE

Annie Clark opened the door to the old-fashioned drugstore. She loved the sound of the tinkling bell hanging from an ancient nail at the corner of the door. For one brief second she wondered if she could steal the little cluster of bells. No, better to tuck the sound into her memory bank.

How she loved this little store. She sniffed as she always did when she entered. The smell was always the same—Max Factor powder, Chantilly perfume, and the mouthwatering aroma of freshly brewed coffee from the counter tucked in between the displays of Dr. Scholl's foot products and the Nature's brand vitamins.

She'd worked here five days a week for the past six years. She knew every item on every shelf as well as the price. Thanks to Elmo Richardson's mother's recipe, she knew how to make and serve the best tuna salad in the world to the students of Boston University. On the days she served cinnamon coffee and the tuna on a croissant, the lines outside the store went around the block. Yes, she was going to miss this place.

As Annie made her way down the aisle, she cast a critical eye over the shelves. Who was going to take her place? Would they love Elmo and the store the way she had? She reached out to straighten a row of Colgate toothpaste boxes.

"Annie! What brings you here today?" the wizened pharmacist asked.

Annie smiled. "I guess I need my drugstore fix for the week. Did you find someone to take my place?"

"I found someone, but he can never take your place, Annie." The pharmacist twinkled. He looked down at the bottle of aspirin in her hand and clucked his tongue. "You won't be taking those tablets after tomorrow, will you?"

"I'll probably be taking more. Just because I'm getting my master's doesn't mean my troubles will be over. I have to find a job and get on with the business of earning a living. One of these days, though, I'm going to start up my own business. You just wait and see. I'm going to miss you, Elmo. You've been more than kind to me all these years."

"I don't understand why you have to leave immediately. Don't you think you've earned the right to sleep in for at least a week? What's the harm in delaying your trip for a few days?"

"The rent is up next week. When I get to Charleston and find a place to live, I'll sleep in for a few days. It's a beautiful day, isn't it, Elmo?"

"One of the prettiest I've seen in a long time. Good weather predicted for tomorrow, too. I'm closing the store to attend your graduation," Elmo said gruffly.

"Really! You're *closing* the store!"

"Yes, and the dean gave me a ticket for a seat in the first row."

Annie walked behind the counter to hug the old man. "I don't know what to say. My brother wrote to say he couldn't make it. Mom doesn't . . . what I mean is . . . oh, Elmo, thank you. I'll be sure to look for you."

"I'm taking you and Jane to dinner afterward. Won't take no for an answer. I might even have a little gift for the two of you." He twinkled again.

Annie laughed. "Don't forget, you promised to write to me. Oh, oh, what's that?" Annie asked, whirling around.

"Backfire. Dang bunch of kids racing their motors is what it is," Elmo grumbled.

Annie pocketed her change. "I'll see you tomorrow, Elmo."

"You bet your boots you'll be seeing me. Go on now. I know this is your sentimental walk before it all comes to an end. Walk slow and savor it all."

Tears welled in Annie's eyes. "I will, Elmo."

"Git now, before you have me blubbering all over this white coat of mine."

"Did I ever tell you that you've been like a father to me, Elmo?"

"A million times. Did I ever tell you you were like a daughter to me, Annie?"

"At least a million times," Annie said in a choked voice.

"Then git!"

Annie fled the store, tears rolling down her cheeks.

She rounded the corner, walked two blocks, sniffling as she went along, before she cut across the campus parking lot. She was aware suddenly of running students, shrill whistles, and wailing police cars. She moved to the side to get out of the way of a careening police car, whose siren was so shrill she had to cover her ears. "What's going on?" she gasped to a young girl standing next to her.

"The cops just shot someone. I think he's dead."

"Was it a student?" Annie crossed her fingers that it wasn't someone she knew.

"I don't know," the girl said in a jittery-sounding voice.

Annie advanced a few steps to stand next to a police officer. "What happened, Officer?"

"Two guys robbed the Boston National Bank. One of them got away, and the other one was shot."

"Oh."

"Move along, miss, and be careful. Until we catch the other guy, don't go anywhere alone and keep your doors locked."

"Yes, yes, I will."

Annie weaved her way among the rows of cars, passing her own Chevy Impala, the bucket of bolts that would hopefully get her to Charleston, South Carolina, the day after tomorrow. Parked right next to her car was Jane's ancient Mustang. She took a moment to realize the windows were open in both cars. Neither she nor Jane ever locked their cars, hoping someone would steal them so they could collect on the insurance. It never happened. She shrugged as she eyed the array of cars. Beemers, shiny Mercedes convertibles, Corvettes, and sleek Buicks. All out of her league. Any car thief worth his salt would go for the Mercedes or the Beemers. She shrugged again as she made her way to the small apartment she'd shared with Jane for the past six years.

Annie opened the door to the apartment and immediately locked it.

"Oh, Annie, you're home. Thank God, I was worried. I just heard on the radio that the bank was robbed. I have three hundred ninety-five dollars in that bank. What's it mean? Is that what all the ruckus is about out there?"

"Yes. I was talking to one of the cops, and he said not to go anywhere alone and to keep our doors locked. One of the gunmen got away. My two hundred eighty dollars is in that bank, too. They're covered by insurance, but I'm taking mine out first thing in the morning. How about you?"

"I think we should go now and do it."

"We can't. The bank is a crime scene now. Tomorrow it will be business as usual. I don't think we have anything to worry about."

Jane Abbott crunched her long, narrow face into a mask of worry as all the freckles on her face meshed together. Her curly red hair stood out like a flame bush as her paint-stained fingers frantically tried to control it. Annie handed her a rubber band. "I'd kill for curly hair," Annie muttered.

"Not this hair you wouldn't. I've been cursed. As soon as we get to Charleston, I'm getting it cut. We're doing the right thing, aren't we, Annie?"

"I think so. We promised ourselves a year to work part-time and to do whatever we wanted before we headed for the business world. It won't be like we aren't working. We proved we can live on practically nothing for the past six years. We can do it for one more year. You're going to paint, and I'm going to serve coffee and tuna sandwiches in a hole in the wall. It is entirely possible we'll become entrepreneurs. We agreed to do this, and we're not switching up now."

Always a worrier, Jane said, "What if our cars conk out?"

"That's why we decided to take both of them and follow each other, remember? If that happens, we ditch one car and transfer our stuff to the other. It's not like we have a lot of stuff, Jane. Clothes and books, that's it. We can do this, I know we can. Guess what, Elmo is coming to our graduation and taking us to dinner. I didn't tell him about the part-time thing or our hope to go into business. He'd just worry about us. He said he might even have a present for us. We'll be just like everyone else who has someone to kiss and hug them when it's all over. We'll be friends forever, won't we, Jane?"

"We lasted six years, so there's no reason we can't last sixty more. That will make us eighty-six, and at that point we probably won't care if we're friends or not."

Annie laughed. "What's for dinner, or are we going to grab a burger and fries?"

"I'm throwing everything in the fridge in one pot. Whatever it turns out to be is what we're having for dinner. Everything's

ready for the new tenant. Sunday morning we'll get up, strip
the beds, and roll out of here as soon as it gets light. Do you
want to pack up our cars tonight or wait till tomorrow night?
Bear in mind that we'll probably be drinking wine with Elmo
tomorrow night. We'll have hangovers Sunday morning. It's
your call, Annie.''

"We can do it after dinner. Instead of taking all our books,
why don't we sell them to the exchange? We can pick up a
few dollars, and it will be less of a load on our springs and
shocks. It will give us more room for your paintings. There's
no way you're leaving those behind. Someday you are going
to be famous and these first paintings of yours are going to be
worth a fortune.''

"I love you, Anna Daisy Clark. You always make me feel
good. We're both going to be famous someday," Jane said,
hugging her friend. "I just hope it's sooner than later.''

"We've worked like Trojans for six years. We held down
jobs, and we're graduating in the top ten percent of our class.
I think that says something for both of us.''

"Don't forget you helped your brother with your mother's
nursing-home bills. I'm sorry she can't be here, Annie.''

A lump formed in Annie's throat. "She'll be here in spirit.
I hope I make enough money someday so I can transfer her to
one of those places that has rolling green lawns and lots and
lots of flower beds. She still loves flowers and gardening. She
has little pots of flowers on the windowsill of her room. Sometimes she forgets to take care of them. I'll be able to visit her
more often so that's a plus.''

"We'll both visit her. If I make more money than you, and
that's probably the joke of the year, I'll help you with her care.
I never knew my parents, so that will make me happy. Is it a
deal, Annie?''

"It's a deal," Annie said solemnly. "You know what, Jane?

I know there's a pot of gold at the end of our rainbow. I just know it.''

"The eternal optimist!'' Jane laughed. "Tell me, are there any red-blooded men at the end of that rainbow?''

"Of course. They're going to sweep us off our feet and make us live happily ever after. Of course I don't know exactly when that's going to happen, but it will happen.'' Annie caught the dish towel Jane threw at her as she made her way to the end of the hall and her bedroom.

In her room with the door closed, Annie allowed her eyes to fill with tears. Tomorrow would be the end of the long road she'd traveled these last six years. The optimism Jane saw was just a facade for her friend's benefit. So many times she'd wanted to give up, to just get a job that paid decent money, to live in a place that didn't crawl with bugs. She was tired of counting pennies, of eating mayonnaise sandwiches, macaroni and cheese, greasy hamburgers and drinking Kool-Aid because it was cheap. At times she resented the mind-boggling monthly sums of money she had to send for her mother's care. Tom had a good job, but he also had three small kids and a demanding wife. He paid what he could. Tom didn't have student loans the way she did. Tom ate steak and roast beef. She hadn't had a steak in two years. How, she wondered, had she managed to survive all these years sleeping just a few hours each night, studying and working? *If you persevere, you will prevail,* she told herself. She'd done just that. One more day, and it would be the first day of the rest of her life. An adventure. And she was ready for it.

God, I'm tired.

Annie woke two hours later when Jane banged on her door, shouting, "Annie Daisy Clark, dinner is now being served!''

"Be right there.''

"This looks, uh . . . interesting," Annie said when she took her place at the table.

"Not only is it interesting, it's delicious. If you don't like the way it tastes, spread the rest of the grape jam over it. At least it will be sweet, and there isn't any dessert. Let's go get an ice-cream cone later. My treat."

"I'd love an ice-cream cone. Shhh, the news is on. Maybe they caught the other guy. I don't know why but that whole thing made me really nervous." Annie's eyes were glued to the small nine-inch television set perched on the kitchen counter.

"Wow! They caught him! Like he really doesn't know where the money is. Do you believe that, Annie?"

"I don't know. There were cops everywhere. They didn't say who was carrying the money, the one they caught or the one that got shot. The campus security team is helping the police so they have a lot of manpower. They'll find it. By tomorrow the money will be safely back in the bank vault. We'll go to the drive-through and close our accounts at eight o'clock when the bank opens. You did good, Jane, this was a decent dinner. I never want to eat macaroni and cheese again as long as I live. You cooked, I'll clean up."

"Do you want to pack up the cars before we go for ice cream or after?"

"Let's do it first. We'll get it out of the way, and we can take a last walk around the campus. It's a beautiful spring night."

"Then that's exactly what we'll do. What did we decide about the books?"

"I called the Book Exchange and someone is coming over to pick them up at nine-thirty. We'll get two hundred and ten dollars. We can stay in a cheap motel one night and not have to worry about making the trip all in one day. How does that sound?"

"Perfect."

"Okay, while you're doing the dishes, I'll go get my car. I can drive yours over, too, if you want me to?"

"That's okay. There are only a few dishes. It's going to take you longer to load your car since you have all those paintings. We'll both finish up at the same time."

An hour later, Annie carried her last suitcase down to the car. Her small carryall with her cosmetics, along with her laundry bag with the bed linens, would be the last thing to go in the car Sunday morning.

"I have some extra room in the backseat if you need it, Jane."

"Do you think you can fit my small easel in there? If you can take it, I'll be able to see out of the rearview mirror."

"Hand it over," Annie said.

"Okay, I'll meet you in the parking lot."

Annie opened the door to shove the easel between the front-passenger seat and the backseat. When the leg of the easel refused to budge, she shoved it with her shoulder. She looked down to see if her old running shoes were in the way. They were, but it was the canvas bag with the black lettering that made her light-headed. Boston National Bank. She swayed dizzily as she lifted the leg of the easel to move it behind the driver's seat. The moment her vision cleared, she rolled up the windows and slammed the car door shut. Another wave of dizziness overcame her as she held on to the door handle for support. When the second wave of dizziness passed, Annie raced into the apartment, where she ran for the bathroom and lost her dinner. She stayed there so long she knew Jane would come looking for her.

Five hundred thousand dollars, the news anchor had said. Two hundred thousand of the five in bearer bonds. Untraceable bearer bonds. In her car. *Call the police. Turn it in,* her brain shrieked over and over. The pot of gold at the end of the rainbow. If she didn't turn it in she could move her mother to a nursing home with rolling green hills and flower beds. She could help her brother Tom. She could set Jane up in a little studio. *Call the police. Turn in the money.*

Annie walked out of the apartment in slow motion, her brain whirling in circles as she contemplated the contents of her car. The bank robber must have thrown it through her open car window when he was running from the police. Surely they searched the area. Would they come back and do a more thorough search? Should she cover it up? Should she pretend she hadn't seen it? What should she do? The pot of gold at the end of the rainbow. Her pot of gold. The news anchor had said the money was in small bills. It wouldn't be traceable. Her battered gym bag found its way to her hands from the trunk of the car. She tossed it on top of the money bag. *No, no, that won't work. If the police do a second search, they might see it in my car and realize that I covered up the money bag. Better to move the gym bag and running shoes to the other side and just toss the easel on top of the money bag. It's dusk. I'll say I didn't look inside. I'll say I just put the easel in and didn't look. How many people look at the floor of the car? I never do. Most people don't. The pot of gold at the end of the rainbow. No one will ever know, not even Jane. I won't tell a soul. Call the police. Turn in the money. I can make Mom's days happier. Tom will be able to spend more time with his wife and kids. Jane needs a chance. Do it. Make a decision. Keep the money or give it back. Keep it or give it back. Yes. No. Call the police. Turn in the money. Decide now before it's too late. Decidedecidedecide. I'm keeping it. No, I'm not. I'm giving it back.*

"Annie. What's wrong? I waited and waited. Then I got scared and decided to come back," Jane said breathlessly. "You look funny. Is something wrong?"

"Kind of. I lost my dinner. I feel kind of wobbly." It was the truth.

"It could be the excitement. I didn't get sick, so it wasn't the food. Stress will do it every time. Do you want to forgo the ice cream and the walk around the campus?"

"No, let's do it. Maybe the ice cream will help. You're probably right, it's stress. I thought it was going to be so easy to walk away from here. We will miss this place." Good God, was this trembly voice hers?

"Any trouble with the easel?"

"No. Actually, there's room to spare. All I have left to put in the backseat is the bedding and my carryall. How about you?"

"I'm crammed to the ceiling but that's okay. Boy, the cops are everywhere. They're checking all the cars on campus. They even went through mine."

"No kidding." Annie thought her heart was going to leap right out of her chest.

"If you don't want them going through all your stuff, leave your car parked here on the street. Just lock it."

"Okay, that sounds good. I probably wouldn't be able to wedge everything in again the way I did the first time."

"Tell me about it. That's what took me so long getting back here. The cop was really nice, though. He said they think there was a third guy, and the one who got shot passed the money to him. Guess it makes sense."

"They didn't say anything about a third man on television."

"It's a theory. If the guy just tossed it, don't you think the cops would have found it by now?"

"Maybe someone found it and kept it," Annie said.

"Are you kidding, Annie? That's a federal rap. No one in their right mind would do something like that. You always get caught in the end."

"Not always. If there was a third person he could be out of

the state by now. If he took a plane, he could be in California.
All he has to do is walk across the border. Think about it,
Jane.''

''Better him than me. I wouldn't want to live the rest of my
life looking over my shoulder.''

''I agree with you. Are they going to search through the
night?''

''I got the impression they're just searching the routes the
two guys took. They're probably done by now. I saw a bunch
of cop cars leaving as I was coming back to get you. Are you
feeling any better?''

''A little. I hope I'm not coming down with something.''

''If you are, Elmo can give you something. We could stop
by after we do our walk.''

''I'll be fine. Tomorrow is our big day. I guess I just never
thought it would get here,'' Annie said, her voice cracking with
the strain.

''Okay, what flavor do you want?''

''Rocky Road. I'm going to sit out here on the bench, okay?''

''Sure. Listen, we can sit here and eat the cones. We don't
have to do the walk if you aren't up to it.''

''I feel better. It's okay, Jane. Stop fussing.''

''If you say so.''

Annie almost jumped out of her skin when one of the campus
police force sat down next to her. ''Evening, Annie.''

''How are you, Kevin?'' Annie asked quietly.

''Tired and hungry. I have to pull a second shift. You want
my opinion, that money is long gone. The only thing that makes
sense is the guy passed it to a third party. When you don't
catch the perp in three hours, it's a lost cause. That's just my
opinion, mind you. What do you think?''

''I think I agree with you. Don't they have *any* clues?''

''I shouldn't be telling you this but no, not a one. They got
the one guy in jail and he says he was just an innocent bystander

that got sucked into this, and he doesn't know anything about the first guy or the third guy. He's sticking to his story, too. They don't share much with us lowly campus police. There's going to be hell to pay because the kid that was shot didn't have any kind of weapon. His father is some Wall Street broker in New York. The other one's father is old money in Boston. Money or not, they'll make an example of the kid. Mark my word. They were best buddies from what I hear, so how could he not know what was going down? Why do rich kids rob banks? Guess I won't be seeing you or Jane after tomorrow, eh?''

"That's right. Sunday morning we're leaving bright and early. It was nice knowing you, Kevin. You take care now. Wait, here comes Jane. I'm sure she'll want to say good-bye."

Annie listened as Jane made small talk with the campus officer. She licked at the dripping ice-cream cone, Kevin's words ringing in her ears.

"Jane, what do you think about leaving right after graduation tomorrow instead of waiting until Sunday morning?" Annie asked.

"What about Elmo?"

"Elmo will understand. We could leave around one and drive for six or seven hours and stop somewhere for the night. We'll treat ourselves to a nice steak house and finish up the trip Sunday. Monday morning we'll start fresh on our new lives."

"That's fine with me. Are you sure you're up to it?"

"I'm sure. Graduation will be over by twelve-thirty. Maybe we could do lunch with Elmo and still be on the road by two o'clock."

"Whatever you want to do, Annie, is fine with me. We need to get back. The guy from the bookstore is supposed to come by at nine-thirty. We can walk some more after he leaves if you want."

"Let's see how we feel," Annie said.

It was close to midnight when Annie closed her bedroom door. She thought about locking it, then wondered where that thought had come from. The word *witness* ricocheted around inside her head. There was always, somewhere, somehow, a witness to everything in life. How could this time be any different? Didn't the police take photographs of the crime scenes? Of course they did. But, was the campus parking lot part of a crime scene? Would her car show up in some photograph with the license plate showing clear as day? Of course it would. Sooner or later they would track down her car through DMV. It wouldn't matter what state she was in. If she could make it to South Carolina, as planned, trade in the car or junk it, hide the money, she would be okay. She was in the drugstore with Elmo when the robbery occurred. She was safe in that regard. She'd walked home. Kevin or one of his colleagues would be able to testify that her car was in the lot. Kevin checked the lot hourly to be sure every car parked had a university sticker on it. He constantly teased her about her bucket of bolts and all the rust on the chrome. Kevin would remember. Kevin knew she and Jane were leaving right after graduation. They'd even talked about it earlier in the week. Yes, lunch with Elmo was necessary. A quick lunch. She really wasn't deviating from her plan.

I guess that means you're planning on keeping the money, her conscience needled.

"I haven't decided," Annie muttered.

Sure you have. You already have it planned out. You need to think about what you'll do if you get caught. Jail time isn't pretty. You'd hate it. You can still call the police. You can turn the money in. Or, you could package it up and send it to them tomorrow morning. The post office is open half a day on Saturdays.

It's my answer to a long list of prayers. Do you have any

*idea how much easier my life will be? I can pay it back at
some point in time. It's for now. Just temporary to get me over
this awful hurdle in my life. I swear to God I'll pay it back.
With interest. I'm a business major. I know how that works. I
can compute interest right down to the last penny. I've never
lied, cheated, or stolen a thing in my life. I've worked harder
than some men. I've always done what's right. I never
begrudged Tom his free education while I had to work for mine.
I pray every night that Mom will get better. She won't, but I
pray anyway. I can make her life more bright, more cheerful.
I can do so much with the money. I'm keeping it!*

Someday you're going to regret it.

*Someday isn't here. This is today and today I won't regret
it. I won't regret it tomorrow or the day after tomorrow, so be
quiet and leave me alone. I need to think.*

What's Jane going to say when she finds out?

*Jane isn't going to find out. Tom isn't going to find out and
neither is my mother. Elmo will never know. Those four people
are the only people in this whole world that are important to
me. The only way they could ever find out is if I tell them. I
didn't even open the damn bag. For all I know it could be
stuffed with paper. The police and the media could be mistaken
about the amount of money.*

*What about the boy's parents? They have money. They'll
hire detectives and detectives sniff around and detectives are
like dogs with bones. Their bonuses depend on results. They'll
love someone like you. Give it back!*

No!

Yes!

Annie bounded off the bed to drag the small slipper chair
to the window. She withdrew her diary, one of many she had
accumulated over the years. She never went to sleep without
writing at least one line about what happened during the day.
Someday, when she was old and gray and sitting in a rocker,

she would show them to her children and grandchildren. For the *zillionth* time she wished her own mother had done the same thing.

Annie wrote carefully, composing the words in her mind first so she could fit them into the three lines afforded this date. *I saw my own personal rainbow today. It's so strange that I was the recipient of this rainbow and no one else. I view it as a personal message that life will be whatever Jane and I choose to make it as we prepare to start our new lives with all our schooling behind us.*

"If anyone reads this, they won't know what I'm talking about," Annie muttered.

She didn't bother to get ready for bed. She knew there would be no sleep for her this night and probably for many nights to come. Instead, she sat on the small tufted chair and watched her car all through the night.

"It was a wonderful lunch, Elmo. Thank you so much. I'm really going to miss you."

"Me too," Jane said in a choked voice. "Promise you'll come to visit."

The old man nodded solemnly. "Maybe in August when I close the store. Things are slow right before the new crop of students arrive. You can call me from time to time, and letters will be welcome. I do love to get letters."

"At least one a week," Annie promised.

"I have a little going-away present for both of you," Elmo said, withdrawing two white envelopes from his inside breast pocket. "Open them."

Both women opened the small envelopes and gasped. "Elmo, this is outrageous. I can't accept this. A thousand dollars is a fortune. No, no, you have to take this back."

"Annie's right, Elmo. This is beyond generous," Jane said.

"Can't. Won't. It's a gift. From my heart. It's going to be hard for the two of you at first. You need rent money, gas money, jobs. Utilities don't come free, you know. How long do you think those ancient vehicles are going to last you? All I want in return is for you to call and write. I don't want to worry about you. Not another word. I have to be getting back to the store now. Call me collect when you arrive. I want your promise."

Both women wrapped their arms around the pharmacist, hugging him until he cried for mercy. "You take care of yourself, Elmo. Remember now, if we ever get married, you promised to give us away."

"Won't forget. Consider it an honor," the old man snapped, his voice gruff and choked. "You git going now before traffic starts building up on the highway."

"My God, Annie, do you believe this?" Jane asked, waving the check in her hand under her friend's nose.

"I love that old man, Jane," Annie said tearfully. "Let's make the trip all in one day. I'm so wired I won't be able to sleep. We can drive through the night and arrive by morning. What do you say? Are you game?"

"Right now, Anna Daisy Clark, I feel like I could fly to South Carolina. Let's hit the road. We will stop for coffee along the way, won't we?"

"Yes. I guess we should just get in our cars and go," Annie said.

"That's a good plan, Annie. Let's do it."

Annie licked at her dry lips. "Yes, let's do it."

CHAPTER TWO

"Tell me again why you wanted to come to this wonderful, warm, sunny place," Jane said as she leaned back in the booth, at the same time pushing her luncheon plate to the middle of the table. "God, I'm tired. You look exhausted, Annie. Both of us need to sleep around the clock."

Annie sighed, a sound that could be heard clear across the room. She lit a stale cigarette, something she rarely did because she couldn't afford to smoke. "My parents used to bring Tom and me here every summer. I remember how happy I was when I got here. My steps were lighter, my face hurt from smiling so much. I clearly remember the early-evening smell of confederate jasmine and sweet olive. I swear, Jane, the scent used to stop me dead in my tracks. My mother always said she wanted to bottle the smell so she would have it nearby once we got back to Tennessee. They call this the low country, and I swear it has a way of creeping into your sleep until even your waking dreams are filled with its spirit and you find yourself in a longing state. I always said I was going to come here and live

someday. Now, I'm here. I hope you're going to love it here
as much as I do."

"I love it already. I don't think I've ever seen such a glorious
array of flowers. What did you say that purple hanging stuff
is?"

"Wisteria. The big bushes are azaleas and the flowering trees
are dogwood. The sweet olive trees are the ones with the little
yellow buds. That was a good lunch, Jane."

"We need to move, Annie, or I'm going to fall asleep. First
stop, the bank, so we can open an account. It's going to take
at least five days for Elmo's check to clear."

"You're right. Thank God we have our apartment. I can't
wait to see it. The landlady said she would have it all ready.
All we have to do is put the sheets on the beds and buy some
groceries. We have a roof over our heads for a month."

Her eyelids drooping, Jane said, "Is our game plan the same?
We get part-time jobs as waitresses while we look for a vacant
shop to open our own business. In the meantime we send out
résumés by the dozen in the hopes someone will snap us up
to add to their payroll or are we going to forget about that for
the time being?"

Annie crawled out of the booth. "I don't think I've ever
been this tired. Let's use the Broad Street Bank for now. Later
on we can change if we want to. For now it will fit our needs.
All the other stuff we'll just play by ear. I'm too tired to think."

It was two-thirty when Annie parked the Impala next to
Jane's Mustang. "Here we are, one-thirty Logan Street. Apartment Seven. The key is under the flowerpot. I'm just carrying
in my bedding. We can unpack the car later."

"I'm with you," Jane said, hauling the canvas laundry bag
from the backseat of her car. "Be sure to lock the doors," she
called over her shoulder.

Annie drew in her breath when she opened the back door of
the Impala. For one heart-stopping moment she wished the

money bag would be gone. She felt faint when she saw it nestled next to one of her running shoes. Surely it was okay to cover it up now. No one had followed them, no one had seemed the least bit suspicious. Maybe she should just throw the bank bag into her laundry bag.´

The moment you do that, you become a thief. A criminal. It's premeditated something or other, she told herself.

I have to move it sometime. The sooner the better. I'm keeping it.

"What are you doing, Annie? I want us both to see our new home at the same moment. Did you lose something?"

"I'm looking for my other running shoe. I found it!" she called as she stuffed the bank bag down deep into her laundry bag. She swore it weighed a thousand pounds as she made her way up the walkway that led to Apartment 7. Guilt was always heavy.

"Okay, open the door, Jane."

"It's not bad," Jane said, looking around. "Actually, it reminds me of the apartment in Boston. It's clean, too. Kitchen is small. Bedrooms are a good size. We can live here comfortably, Annie. I can spruce it up once we get settled."

"The rent is good, it's a quiet little street. I like it that we're close to King Street. That's where all the shops are. We might even be able to get around on foot if our cars give out. Which bedroom do you want?"

"I'll take the one without the wallpaper. Cabbage roses make me dizzy. I'm going to say good night, Annie."

"There's a grocery store on Rutledge. First one up buys the groceries. I expect we'll sleep until tomorrow. Night, Jane."

Annie closed the door. She felt a surge of panic when she saw there was no lock on it. Maybe that was good. The bank bag went under the bed in the blink of an eye. Sooner or later she was going to have to open it. "Later rather than sooner," she mumbled as she whipped out sheets and a light summer blanket. Ten minutes later she was sound asleep.

Annie woke thirteen hours later to the smell of coffee and frying bacon. She realized she was ravenous. "Guess you got up first, huh?" she said, shuffling into the kitchen.

"Sure did. The shower leaves a lot to be desired, but the water was hot. I got everything at this neat little store. We need to find a real grocery store. That one was expensive."

"What time is it?"

"It's eleven o'clock. If you don't dilly-dally, we can be out of here by one. By the way, the phone is hooked up. Do we have anyone to call?"

"Not a soul. This is so good, Jane. Why is it I eat three eggs every morning and you only eat one?"

"Because I am a one-egg person. Maybe someday I will eat three. There's a first time for everything."

Annie felt her heart thump in her chest. It was true, there was a first time for everything. Every criminal did something wrong for the first time. The word *criminal* drained the color from her face.

"You look kind of peaked, Annie. Are you sure you're feeling okay?"

"I'm fine. Maybe I got too much sleep. You know, everything is so new and yet not new if you know what I mean. It was a great breakfast. Do you mind cleaning up?"

"No. Take as long as you need."

Annie bolted for her room. On her hands and knees, she dragged the money bag out to the middle of the floor. Her hands trembling, she undid the metal clasp and dumped the contents on the floor. Loose bills of every denomination, slender packets of bills, and the crinkly bearer bonds littered the floor. She scooped it all into a pillowcase and stuffed it back into the laundry bag. At some point she was going to have to burn the bag and toss the clasp into the ocean just on the off chance that the clasps on the money bags were identical to the bank's logo or crest. At the last second, she pulled out two hundred dollars in twenty-dollar bills. She would need deposit monies at some point. Better not to keep going into the bag.

Anna Daisy Clark, you are now a bona fide criminal. A thief of the first order. If you get caught, you will go to jail. I'm not going to get caught. This is for now. I'm going to pay it back as soon as possible. I'm not just saying that. I will pay it back. I promise.

That's what every thief in the world says when they find themselves behind bars, her conscience needled.

Annie ignored the voice inside her head as she stepped into the shower. Glorious, hot, steaming water pelted her naked body. She washed her hair twice and lathered her body three times before she was ready to leave the little cubicle.

She towel-dried her hair, having no idea where her blow-dryer was. She thanked God again as she always did for her wash-and-wear hair. Dressed in wrinkled chinos, worn sandals, and a tank top, she stood back to survey herself in the blurry mirror. For today it would do.

The diary was in her hands almost before she knew it. She wrote quickly, wanting her small confession condensed in as few words as possible. *We arrived in Charleston yesterday and slept for thirteen hours. All is secure.*

Annie closed the diary with a loud snap. The two hundred dollars went into the pocket of her chinos.

"Where to?" Jane asked.

Annie rummaged in her purse for the small notebook she was never without. "I thought we would apply for jobs at Hyman's first. Then we can check out this list of available storefronts the Chamber of Commerce sent me. I don't have a clear memory of the places on the list. We stopped coming here when I was around fourteen or so, and I'm sure things have changed. There's a map, though, so we'll be able to get around easily.''

At three-thirty, both women had the promise of temporary part-time waitressing jobs. ''Eight hours a week if the tips are good is okay,'' Annie assured Jane. ''It will get us over the hurdle if we can't find a location to open a business. This one on George Street looks pretty good. It's smack-dab in the middle of the Charleston campus and will draw students. Bishop England High School is close, so that's a plus. Let's go there first and see what we can work up if anything. According to this map the building is between King and Phillips. Do you think we should call the broker first?''

Jane snorted. ''Do you know who the broker is?''

''No. Okay, let's go. It can't be far. If it looks promising, we can call the broker from a phone booth.''

It was almost five-thirty when Annie pressed her nose up against the grimy storefront window. ''It's a dump, that's for sure. Do you think it's *doable,* Jane?''

''*Doable* as in Annie and Jane doing all the work. I don't know, Annie. I need to see the inside. It's big. For some reason I thought it would be, you know, little, kind of like a big walk-in closet. I saw a phone booth down the street. I'll call. In the meantime, go into that store next to it and ask some questions. It looks like it's been empty for a long time.''

Annie's brain whirled as she moved along the wide front windows to rub at the grime. All things considered, it would be perfect for what she and Jane had in mind. There was even a counter.

''He's coming right over,'' Jane said. ''What did you find out?''

''Nothing. The man was locking up. I didn't want to bother him. If the rent is right, this might work, Jane. Look, there's a counter. My end would be here, yours to the right. Once these windows are cleaned you'd have really good light. Coffee by Annie and paintings by Jane. I'm liking this more and more. Cross your fingers that the rent is something we can handle. Do you think that's a cash register?''

"It looks like one to me. I guess this is Mr. Peabody coming toward us. He said his office was just a block away. He doesn't look like a shark, does he?''

"All real-estate people are sharks. Stay alert. Go across the street and ask the music people how long this place has been empty."

"Anna Clark, and you must be Mr. Peabody," Annie said, holding out her hand. The Realtor's hand was moist and clammy. Annie fought the urge to wipe her own hand on her chinos. Instead she jammed both her hands into her pockets.

Peabody was round like a melon. Even his face was round, with a goatee. He looked to Annie like a benevolent barracuda listing to the left. He removed his Panama hat with a flourish, revealing a shiny bald head that was wet with sweat. A massive ring of keys appeared in his hands. She watched as he fit key after key into the lock until finally he found the right one.

"Wonderful location. Right in the heart of things. You couldn't want anything better. A little paint will work wonders. The other shopkeepers are just wonderful people. Neighborly, if you know what I mean. They help one another. You ladies aren't from around here, are you?''

"You mean are we *Yankees?* Actually, Mr. Peabody, I am Anna Clark, and my friend is Jane. That's who we are."

"Lord love a duck. You young women today say the goldang-est things."

Jane returned to the shop holding up two fingers and then whacked the first finger at the second knuckle, meaning the store had been empty for two and a half years. Annie's brain buzzed.

"How much is the rent, Mr. Peabody?" she asked.

"Seven hundred and fifty dollars."

Annie laughed. Jane joined in. Annie's brain continued to buzz as she tried to calculate rent for two and a half years. Somewhere in the neighborhood of $23,000.

Peabody's voice was unctuous sounding. "Does the amount offend you ladies?"

Annie squared her shoulders. She was a business major. She should be able to handle this in a mature, professional manner. "Let's cut the bullshit, Mr. Peabody. This store has been empty for two and a half years. At the price you quoted, you lost approximately twenty-three thousand dollars. My friend and I are willing to pay three hundred a month providing you do certain things. Mainly clean up this dump and take out all this trash. A paint job goes with the deal. We're willing to sign a three-year lease and a renewal at the end of three years with a fifty-dollar increase. It won't do to haggle. It's all we can afford, so it's a take-it-or-leave-it offer."

Peabody mopped at his glistening bald head. "I need to think about this."

"So think," Annie said smartly. "When we walk out of here the deal is off the table. Don't think about asking us for a security deposit because we can't afford it. However, we can possibly work out something where we could pay something every month toward a month's rent as security. Tell me, does the plumbing work in the bathroom and the sink behind the counter. If it doesn't, it will have to be fixed. What was in this store before?"

"Homemade candies, crafts, gifts, that sort of thing. The Hobart ladies were here for eighteen years before they closed up."

"Do you really expect me to believe the Hobart ladies paid you seven hundred and fifty dollars a month selling homemade candies, Mr. Peabody?" Annie asked, her voice ringing with disdain.

"My memory could be off a little. I'm not as young as I used to be," Peabody said. His handkerchief was soaking wet.

"Does that mean we have a deal?"

Peabody hedged. "When would you want to take possession?"

"The minute this dump passes inspection. Electric, plumbing, paint job, trash removal. The cash register stays, as does the counter and those two round tables and chairs."

"Now, I don't know about that, Miss Clark."

Annie was in the man's face a moment later. "What don't you know, Mr. Peabody? That has to be part of the deal. It's after six, Mr. Peabody, and we've had a very long day. I'd like a handshake agreement until we can have a lawyer draw up a lease we're all happy with. What's it going to be?"

"Well, all right. I know I'm going to regret this at some point, but it's a deal. There's a young lawyer in town, Robert Rose, who can handle the lease. I've never used his services so we'll be neutral in that respect. If we're both agreeable, I don't see the need to engage two attorneys."

"That's fine with us. I'll call for an appointment. We'll split the fee and tell him we don't consider it a conflict of interest for him to represent both of us. If we can, we can set it up for tomorrow or the day after. In the meantime, I'd like to leave a deposit of two hundred dollars. In cash. It shows our good faith."

"Certainly, certainly. What are you ladies going to be doing here? I guess I should have asked earlier."

"Coffee," Annie said, counting out the two hundred dollars from her pocket. She pretended not to see the surprise on Jane's face. She shot her a warning look that said I'll explain later.

"When do you think the repairs will be done, Mr. Peabody?"

"By the end of the week. You'll have the weekend to set things up the way you want them. I don't like that part about the extended lease after three years," Peabody fretted.

Annie snatched the money back from his hand. Peabody grabbed for it saying, "I just said I didn't like it. I didn't say I wouldn't go along with it."

"You need to write that down on the back of the receipt," Annie said coldly. "I don't want this coming back to slap me in the face later on."

"You certainly do drive a hard bargain. You've got to be a *Yankee.*"

"Mr. Peabody, I am Anna Clark. Let's put that to rest right now."

Peabody sucked in his fat cheeks. "It's resting."

Annie held out her hand. Peabody hesitated a moment before reaching for it. Annie squeezed hard. Jane did the same thing, smiling all the while.

"The key, Mr. Peabody. Jane and I want to walk around, take measurements, that kind of thing. I think two hundred dollars is sufficient for the key. We'll lock up when we leave. I'm sure you have an extra, don't you?"

"Yes, yes, of course. It's someplace back in the office. I'll say good night then, ladies."

Annie and Jane whooped their joy the moment the door closed and Peabody was across the street.

"Lord, girl, I didn't know you had it in you!" Jane said. "This dump is worth at least four hundred dollars."

"Time will tell. It's ours, and that's all that matters. I know you're dying to know where I got that two hundred dollars. You aren't going to believe this. It was in my gym bag. Remember when we were saving for that television we were going to put in the living room? We finally gave up on the idea. I guess both of us just forgot about it. Good thing I found it, huh?"

Not only are you a crook, a thief and a criminal but you're a liar as well. You just lied to your best friend. See how easy it is to go off the straight and narrow?

Annie gave herself a mental shrug, her breath exploding in

a hissing sound. *Yes, damn it, I am all those things but I'm not going to think about it now. I am going to pay it back, every single cent plus interest. Absolutely I am going to do that.* Her shoulders felt incredibly heavy as she followed Jane around the spacious shop. The word *felon* found its way into her head just as Jane said, "Take a good look at this counter. It's solid oak. Oak is such a beautiful wood. Why would someone paint it? Let's strip and refinish it, Jane."

"Sure, but we can't do that until all the dust settles. The floor has to be sanded. Damn, we didn't put that on the list for Peabody. Maybe for the time being we can just wash it real good and put some kind of wax on it. Or hire someone to clean it, buff it, and polish it with that shiny stuff they use today. It's heart of pine and durable as hell. The boards are even, no sagging anywhere. Let's not spend any money we don't have to spend. Do you think it's possible to rent a sewing machine around here, Annie?"

"That's why they have Yellow Pages. I would think so. Why?"

"Take a look at those windows. They're just crying for something cheerful. I could make them. If we can fit some material into our budget, I can buy some great fabric and some sailcloth to make an awning for over the front door. There's something quaint and homey about an awning. Don't ask me what it is, it just is. I could paint daisies and sunflowers all over it. White muslin for the curtains with the same hand-painted flowers. For some reason people just seem to home in on things like that. I can redo those two tables and cover the seats with the same muslin. I bet we could find a bench to put outside the door, too. Little things like that for eye appeal. We have to get them in the door."

"We're going to need a catchy name for this place," Annie said, her shoulders lightening imperceptibly. "Something we can both relate to. Something that takes in my coffee and your painting. You can make the sign, can't you?''

"Sure, and the chains are still hanging outside. I could make it in the form of a daisy or a sunflower, or how about a rainbow?''

Annie choked on her own saliva. Jane thumped her on the back. "You okay?''

"I just swallowed wrong. None of them sound professional. We need something with some zip to it. We'll think of something tonight.''

"I'm really psyched about this, Annie. I'm disappointed, though. I thought you'd be just as excited. It's not as though we haven't talked about this for years.''

"I guess it's the financial end of things that's spooking me.''

"You!'' Jane scoffed. "You're the girl who makes things happen, the girl who knows how to squeeze a nickel eight different ways, the girl who can make a six-course dinner out of nothing and have it taste good. You!''

Annie laughed. "We're going in three different directions. We agreed to waitress part-time. We're sending out résumés for full-time jobs. Now this. I know it was part of our grand plan, but how are we going to do it all now? What if we don't make a profit? Think about the bills.''

Jane planted her hands on her bony hips. "You're starting to scare me, Annie. Look, we don't have to waitress. We don't have to send out résumés. We can tackle this and hope for the best. I'm for whatever will take that awful look off your face. This is supposed to be a happy time for us.''

"You know what, Jane, you are absolutely right. Let's go home, unpack the cars, go out to dinner to that big steak we promised ourselves, and really talk this through. Look, if things start to get sticky, I can always ask Elmo for a loan. I'm sure he'd give it to us. I think it's not having a cushion to fall back on in case things are lean for a while,'' Annie said.

"We aren't going to think about that. I like it when you're being the eternal optimist and I'm the pessimist."

Annie shivered. "Then that's the way it's going to be," she said, linking her arm through Jane's. "Come on, let's lock up *our* shop and head home. We have a home now, you know."

"Good idea," Jane said.

On Monday, June 6, 1980, the Daisy Shop opened for business. There was no advance notice, no fanfare, and no publicity because the owners couldn't afford it. No one was more surprised than the owners at the steady stream of customers. Jane said it was because of the daisy-patterned awning. Annie said it was Elmo's mother's tuna fish sandwiches that were served from twelve to one.

By four o'clock, they had gone through ten pounds of coffee and 150 tuna sandwiches. By four-thirty they had to tell disappointed customers they had to close to restock. The groans and moans were music to their ears.

In the small storage room at the back of the shop, the two women danced and twirled in glee. "Do you think it will be like this every day, Jane?"

"God, I hope so. I sold, are you ready for this, eighty-five hand-painted postcards of this shop at three bucks a pop. Annie, that is two hundred forty-nine dollars. I know that isn't going to happen every day, but tourists will still come in. If I sell twenty or twenty-five a day it will keep me in paints and cards. I sold two eight-by-tens for forty dollars each. We covered half the rent with just that alone. God, you were so right. This is going to work. The students loved it. How many requests did you have for espresso and latte?"

"I lost track. I never thought the tuna would go over like it did. We have to call Elmo tonight and tell him. He'll be so tickled. It's all so wonderful, Jane. Everything is so fresh, so clean and pretty. You want to bet tomorrow *jams.*"

"Does that mean we're going to be making tuna all night?"

"It means we have to go to Harris Teeter for coffee—vanilla, hazelnut, and cinnamon. Twenty pounds, Jane! Say it out loud!"

"Twenty pounds!" Jane giggled. "I can't wait to count the money."

"We're going to need a supplier. We can't keep running to the supermarket and paying full price. That eats into our profits. Elmo can tell us how to go about all that. We need to buy wholesale. You should think about that for your supplies, too, Jane."

"Oh, I will. I think God smiled on us today, Annie."

Annie's exuberance died at Jane's words. She turned away so Jane wouldn't see her miserable face.

"Phone's ringing, Annie. You're the closest."

Annie picked up the phone. "Tom! Oh, Tom, wait till I tell you! We sold out. We actually had to close up shop. You did call to congratulate me, didn't you? What's wrong?" Annie listened, her eyes filling with tears. "That can't be, Tom. The place was clean. We both checked it out. There was ample help. Mom wouldn't . . . there are no animals there. Is the doctor sure? Oh, God! Tom, I'm living in a tiny two-bedroom apartment. I can't take care of her. I would if I could. Couldn't you convert your garage until I have this place up and running? You could make two nice rooms for Mom and Social Services would send someone to watch her. I can't do it all, Tom. I just can't. Look, I worked three part-time jobs, put myself through school, while all that was handed to you. Maybe you need to think about *that.* I, personally, don't give a good rat's ass what Mona wants, Tom. It's just for a little while until I can get things together. I'll take care of Mom then. Can't you at least meet me halfway?" Annie blinked when she heard the sound of the dial tone. She felt sick to her stomach at what she was about to do. With her finger on the bar so Jane couldn't hear the dial tone she said, "How much money and how soon can you send it? That much? Fine, Tom. Okay, I'll call the nursing home and the doctor. I'll find a nice place for Mom here. Of course I'll pay my share. So I'll have to moonlight if I need to. I've done it before. Fine, fine, I'll let you know."

"What is it, Annie? What happened?" Jane asked, putting her arms around her friend. Just then, the shop bell rang, but neither woman noticed.

"Tom said . . . what he said was . . . what the doctor told him was Mom got bitten. On both her legs. The doctor said it was from a . . . raccoon. She wasn't the only one either. Mom said it was a kitten. She would think that in her condition. They're going to keep her in the hospital for a few days, then send her back to the nursing home. I just don't understand. It was clean, well maintained, a good staff. The food looked appetizing. Mom seemed to like it. It wasn't the prettiest place in the world, but it was the best we could do at the time. Tom wants me to bring Mom here. He even gave me the name of a place that sounds wonderful. He's going to send some money. He didn't say how much, though." Annie burst into tears.

"Now what am I supposed to do?" Annie wailed.

"I'll tell you what you're going to do, young lady. You're going to pull up your socks and do what you're supposed to do. Go get your mother and bring her here."

"Elmo! What are you doing here?" Annie and Jane squealed in unison.

"Came for the grand opening! Damn plane got stuck in Roanoke and had to wait for six hours. Could have walked here in that time. Blow your nose. I hate a sniffling woman."

"Did you close the store?"

"Hell no, I didn't close the store. I sold the damn thing."

"You sold the drugstore?" Jane and Annie said in amazement. "You love that store. You said you would never sell it."

"I did say that. I happen to love you girls more. I missed you. Got twice as much as the store was worth, too. I'm moving here to keep my eye on you two. Seems like I arrived at just the right moment."

"We were going to call you tonight, Elmo. Everyone liked your mother's sandwiches. We sold out."

"Knew you would. Let's sit down here and palaver. My daddy used to say that. Never had the occasion to use that word until now. The way I see it is we're faced with a crisis. I'm good in a crisis. Real good. I worked behind the counter at the store for years. Filled prescriptions, sold toothpaste, cleaned the place at the end of the day. I think I can serve coffee and sandwiches while you go for your mama. You look into that place your brother mentioned. If she don't care for it, she can move in with me when I get my place. I'm just itching to spend that money I got from the sale of the store. Is this all getting through to you, Annie?"

"Yes. Elmo, Mom doesn't know any of us. She lives in her own little world. She wanders off and can't remember her name or where she belongs. She needs constant care. This is all so wonderful of you, but I can't let you do it."

"Don't have much else to do now, do I?"

"Well . . . are you sure, Elmo?"

"Child, I am sure. I wouldn't be here otherwise. I missed you two girls so much I couldn't wait to make my plane reservation. I'm here. That says it all. I'm sleeping on your couch tonight until I can find my own place."

Annie blew her nose again. "You're right, Elmo, that says it all."

"This is a classy little store. Not the best neighborhood, but maybe the rest of the shopkeepers will update a little. Good crowd today, eh?"

"Jane sold eighty-five hand-painted postcards and two eight-by-tens. She sat right there and painted them for the customers. They loved it. How are things back in Boston? Did they ever find the money those guys took off with?"

"No. They must have been in my store six or seven times. Insurance people, cops, detectives, lawyers, and even a private detective. Did they ever call you? When I told them you were talking to me and buying aspirin they asked for your address and phone number. Jane's, too. Don't know why. Told them all we heard was a backfire that turned out to be a gunshot. The trail is stone cold. They're never going to find that money. The third guy is probably sunning himself on some South Sea island. Newspapers are saying the boy in jail is going to get twenty years. Pity."

"Yes it is. You were right, Elmo, when you said open near a campus, and you won't go wrong."

"Maybe we need to think about expanding. This is a big state."

"Elmo, I just opened. Today could be a fluke. Business will taper off in the summer when the students leave."

"Summer school, tourists, regulars. Might see a slight dip, but it's only two and a half months out of the year. My store was always down in summer but it evened out in the fall. You take the good with the bad and work with it. You don't stock heavy during that time. We'll work it out. You girls did real well. What'd it cost you?"

"Rent's three hundred. It cost us seventy-five to get the floor in shape. It's heart of pine. If we keep up with it, we should be able to save it, heavy traffic and all. Jane rented a sewing machine and made the awning and the curtains. She did the murals and painted the tables and chairs. That all came to a hundred. Ten bucks to rent the sewing machine. We stripped and varnished the counter ourselves. That was another twenty dollars. We're leasing a refrigerator. We can't cook here, so

we're just going to serve sandwiches and maybe brownies one
day a week. It's all we can handle. We do need to buy wholesale,
though.''

''You certainly do. Do you think we could go out to dinner,
ladies? I haven't eaten all day, and my mouth is watering for
some of those fat Southern shrimp I hear so much about. It
will be my treat. We can talk about your mother and business
over a nice glass of wine.''

''We accept, don't we, Jane?''

''I love you, Elmo Richardson,'' Jane said, wrapping her
arms around the old man.

''Me too,'' Annie said.

Everything was going to be just fine now. Or was it just
wishful thinking on her part? A chill ran up Annie's spine
when she recalled Elmo's words about all the people who had
questioned him. Would those same people think it suspicious
that he sold out right after the robbery and moved here to be
with Jane and her? Probably. Elmo would put them in their
place lickety-split. Thank you, God, for sending Elmo. I wish
I knew why You're being so good to me after what I did.

''Lock the door, Annie.''

''Okay. It does look pretty, doesn't it?''

''Just like my postcards,'' Jane laughed.

''And I have the two prettiest girls in town going out to
dinner with me. Who could want more?'' Elmo said.

Who indeed? Annie thought.

CHAPTER THREE

"Dr. Mitchum, are you sure Mom is up to the trip?"

"Annie, your mother is right as rain. The bites have healed nicely. She had no adverse effects from the drugs. The raccoon was tested, and it wasn't rabid. She was lucky. Tall Pines is a wonderful nursing home. I don't think your mother will be taking any more naps in a woodshed anytime soon. It was a freak accident."

"That's just the point. Mom shouldn't have been allowed to wander off. However, I understand what you're saying. She used to do a lot of gardening, and we did have a toolshed where she kept all her potting tools and such. Maybe she thought she was back home. This is just a guess on my part, but she might have thought the raccoon was our old cat Flossie."

"Sometimes there's a little spark, Annie. Not often. Your mother can be quite vibrant at times. I've taken care of everything with Tall Pines. Norma is free to go whenever you're ready. I'm truly sorry this happened."

"Me too, Dr. Mitchum. In a way it is probably a good thing.

I'll be able to visit more often and take her on outings. Guess I'll say good-bye. Thanks for taking such good care of Mom.''

Annie was almost to the door when the kindly doctor called her name. ''Annie, always be kind to your mother. Even though she's in her own little world, she has feelings and anxiousness. Lately she's been crying a lot. We don't know why. I just wanted you to know that.'' Annie nodded.

Annie pasted a tired smile on her face when she rounded the corner to enter the visitor's lounge. Her mother was pacing, a nurse's aide alongside her.

''Ready, Mom?''

Norma Clark looked around, a confused look on her face. ''Are you speaking to me, child?''

''Yes. I'm Annie. We're going to go for a ride.''

''I don't think so. Not today. I'd just like to go home.''

''Okay, then let's go home.''

''That's very kind of you. What did you say your name was?''

''Anna Daisy Clark,'' Annie said with a catch in her voice.

''That's a very pretty name. Were you named after a flower? I used to have daisies in my garden. I planted them myself.''

''I know. I used to pick them for you.''

''My goodness, I don't remember that.''

''Careful now. The car is right over there. Do you want to sit in the front or the back?''

''It's a short ride, so it doesn't matter.''

''Mom, it's a long ride. Six hours or so. Front or back? There's a pillow in the back.''

''That's just like your father. He always thought I needed a pillow. How did you get here, Annie?''

''Mom, you know me?'' Annie asked incredulously.

''Of course I know you. Anna Daisy Clark. Sometimes I used to call you Lazy Daisy when you didn't clean your room.''

''Oh, Mom,'' Annie said tearfully. ''This is the best thing

that's happened to me in a long time. Tom is going to be so happy when I tell him.''

"Who's Tom?'' Norma asked as she climbed into the backseat.

Annie's clenched fist hit the side of the door with such force, pain ricocheted up and down her arm. *This must be one of the little sparks Dr. Mitchum was talking about,* she thought as she settled herself behind the wheel. *A spark is good. I'll settle for a spark once in a while. Thank you, God, for that one. I promise not to be greedy.*

Annie chattered nonstop for the first half of the trip. It wasn't until they stopped for coffee and gas that she withdrew the last piece of the metal lock from the money bag in her purse while her mother was using the rest room. She'd hacked it to pieces back in Charleston and now she was leaving a piece of it wherever she stopped. This last piece she planned on throwing out the window in the first rural area she came to. She'd burned the canvas bag the night she'd left. In the middle of the night she'd scattered the ashes all along Rutledge Street.

Norma Clark tapped Annie's arm. "Young lady, we're never going to get home if you stand there staring off into space. What is it you do besides driving ladies home?''

Annie felt her throat tighten up. "I have a coffee shop. I sort of, kind of, robbed a bank, Mom.''

"Mercy, child. Whatever did you do that for? Are you poor?''

"Dirt-poor. I thought I did it for you. That's probably a lie because I used two hundred dollars of it for a rent deposit. I'm going to put that back, though. You know what, Mom, it all just closed in on me. There it was, right in front of me. I took it. It's a really long story. I have all this money now and I'm not sure what I should do. Then the call came about you from Tom. It was almost like it was meant to be. I know it wasn't, but that's how it felt,'' Annie babbled. "Then Elmo came, and he offered to help. He sold his store to come here with Jane and me. He needs someone, too. Everyone needs someone, Mom.''

"Young lady, why do you keep calling me Mom. Do I remind you of your mother?''

The knot in Annie's throat grew in size as she struggled with the words. "You . . . you look just like her. She was always so pretty, just like you. She made the best peanut butter cookies. Her tulips were the prettiest ones on the street. Especially the purple ones.''

"I remember those. I ordered the bulbs from Holland. They were so beautiful. Your father wouldn't let me pick them. He used to count them when he came up the walkway. Why isn't your father here? Is his arthritis bothering him again?''

Another little spark. "I love you, Mom. God, how did this happen?''

"Goodness, Annie, watch where you're driving before you kill us both. Are we about home now?''

"Soon," Annie said tearfully. "Do you love me, Mom?''

"Goodness sakes, child, I don't even know you. I'm sure when I get to know you better I'll love you.''

Annie drove in silence, tears rolling down her cheeks.

Annie felt soft pats on her shoulder. "Now, now, it will all work out. Don't cry. If I could just remember what it was I said to make you cry, I would apologize.''

"Don't worry about it. I'm not crying anymore. Now I'm mad. Your son Tom is a shit. And you know what else? His wife Mona is an even bigger shit. Right now I don't like either one of them. You know, Mom, I never complained. Not once. I worked my ass off, I really did. Tom got everything handed to him. You'd think he'd want to help or at least offer. Is it because I'm a daughter, and he's a son? That's why I did what I did. I'm not a thief. Well, I am, but I wasn't before. I turned into a liar, too. Are you ashamed of me, Mom?''

Norma Clark clamped her lips shut, then opened them. "I won't tell a soul about your secrets."

Annie took her eyes off the road long enough to turn around and say, "If you do, I'll go to jail. They'll lock me up and throw away the key."

Norma Clark's shoulders stiffened. "That's what they do to me. They lock me in my room. It's the same thing as jail. People steal my clothes and my shoes. I never tell. I don't want to get punished."

Annie's foot hit the brake as she steered the car to the side of the road. There was outrage in her voice when she said, "Did they punish you?"

"Yes. They didn't let me go out among the flowers. They even tied Grace in her chair. I untied her," Norma said defiantly. "We didn't get any dinner. They always slapped Grace because she wouldn't listen."

"Oh, God," Annie said.

"I used to pray that my daughter would come and get me. She never did."

Annie let the tears flow. "When we get home you can write to Grace," she managed to say.

"Grace is dead," Norma said flatly.

Was this real? Did her mother know what she was talking about? Was this all some figment of her imagination? "Oh, God, oh, God," Annie wailed.

"It's too late to cry," Norma said.

"When did Grace die, Mom?"

"A long time ago. Maybe it was yesterday. Sometimes I can't remember. Don't tell anyone."

Annie felt light-headed. "I won't tell anyone about Grace if you don't tell anyone I took the money."

Norma's head bobbed up and down. "That sounds fine to me. Should we shake hands?"

"Why the hell not," Annie muttered as she extended her

hand. Norma pumped it vigorously. "How did Grace die, Mom?"

"They punished her and she died. Billie said we have to mind our p's and q's or the same thing will happen to us. I mind my p's and q's," Norma said primly.

Annie turned around and took a deep breath. "I don't think we should talk about this anymore. Let's talk about something nice." She made a mental note to find out who Billie was.

"This certainly is the long way home. Did you take a wrong turn, young lady?"

"More than one. Why don't you take a nap on that nice pillow. I'll wake you when we get home. Mom, do you remember that frilly flowered dress, the one with the purple and pink flowers? You had a sun hat with a big purple ribbon on it that you used to wear in the garden."

"I told you, young woman, they steal all my things."

"I'm going to buy you one just like it," Annie said. "No one is ever going to steal your things again. I promise."

When Annie looked in the rearview mirror she saw that her mother was sound asleep. "Goddamn it, I will not cry. I absolutely will not cry. I am so sorry, Mom. I did the best I could. Even Tom did the best he could at the time. I thought we were on top of things. I really did. From now on you are going to be safe and happy. I don't care what that makes me." To make her point, Annie leaned her head out the window and shouted at the top of her lungs, "Do you hear me? I don't give a good goddamn what that makes me. I don't care if I go to jail. I don't care if I fry in hell. So there, damn it!"

Norma Clark slept deeply and soundly during her daughter's tirade.

Annie woke while it was still dark outside. It was her day to open the shop for the early-morning coffee trade. She was bone tired, but, as she put it, it was a good kind of tired. Elmo had arranged for Norma to be looked after by two women until there was an opening at the Westbury Center. He had been delighted when he described the facility, saying each resident had his or her own apartment with a small walled garden. Security, he went on to say, was high-tech with a twenty-four-hour monitoring system. The part he liked best, he said, was that patients with Norma's condition wore a decorative bracelet that allowed the orderlies to know where they were at all times. The grounds contained a pool, a hot tub, a small petting zoo, a tennis court, as well as a basketball court. A community room with a fully stocked library, a sixty-inch television, and a stereo system rounded out the amenities. The bottom line, Elmo said, was, "It's not as expensive as you might think. With Norma's social security and the part of your father's pension that reverted to her, you and Tom only have to pay two thousand dollars a month. That's just six hundred more than what you were paying in Raleigh. With things going the way they are, I think you can handle it, Annie."

"I can't count on Tom, Elmo. Tom said Mona refuses to pay another nickel. He's got three kids, and he's already holding down a part-time job at night. For now, I have to pay the whole thing."

"You've made a pretty penny since opening day. This is just a guess on my part, but I think you're going to have to hire a few part-timers. The two nights we stayed open till nine were very profitable. However, I'm the first to admit that five in the morning till ten at night isn't a pace anybody can keep up with. When you own your own business, you're married to it. I'm the living proof. When you're dealing with a cash business, you need honest people working for you. Like you and Jane when you worked for me. I lost money over the years with help that thought my money was theirs. Among the three of us, we'll work something out."

"I hope so, Elmo, because I'm starting to get nervous. I never expected anything even half as successful as this. This is just short of phenomenal."

"I know, Annie. If you opened other stores on other campuses like this one, they'd be just as successful. When this one is truly off the ground, you might want to think about it. You started this one on a shoestring, and look what happened. If you need an investor, I'm yours for the taking."

"Elmo, I can't even think about that yet."

"You have to think about it, Annie. We've sold out every single day we've been open. Would you listen to me. I sound like I'm part of this."

"You are!" Jane and Annie said in unison.

"You get up when we do," Annie went on. "You make coffee, boil milk, make sandwiches just like we do. That makes you a one-third partner."

"I don't want to be a partner. My business days are over. I only want to help. I get a kick out of talking to the kids. They call me Pops, can you beat that?"

Annie laughed. "They called you Pops back in Boston, too."

"Speaking of Boston, I got a form letter today that was forwarded from that same insurance company asking me to make a list of all the people I knew who frequented my store that day and any personal information I might have. I tore it up. They're getting to be a pain in my behind. I think they're desperate is what I think."

"I think I hate insurance companies as much as I hate used-car salesmen. They want their premiums, and when it's time to pay out they fight you every step of the way. On top of that they then raise your rates. If I get one, I'm tearing up mine, too," Jane said.

"Yeah, me too," Annie said quietly.

"I did a watercolor the other day of a Charleston garden,

Annie. Do you want to take it to your mother? I know she loves flowers. I just put a plain white frame on it.''

"She'll love it," Annie said.

"You sound funny. Are you okay?"

"I'm getting a headache. I used to get headaches when I didn't know if I could make the rent and buy food. Now, when things are going well, I'm worried it won't last. I guess I'm going to have to go back on my aspirin kick again. By the way, Jane, did we leave a forwarding address?"

Jane slapped at her forehead. "Damn, I forgot. I was going to do it the day of the bank robbery, then you came home and I forgot. I can send one of those forms to the post office tomorrow. I'm sorry, Annie."

"Don't do it for me. All our bills were paid. Tom has this address. Mom isn't in that nursing home anymore, so who would write me? Forget it."

"Okay, I will. Well, I'm going to pack up my gear and head home. It's my turn to cook. How about stuffed pork chops?"

"Make me two," Elmo said smartly.

"Me too," Annie said just as smartly. No forwarding address meant the insurance company couldn't locate her or Jane. *Thank you, God.*

"Annie, I forgot to tell you something. Your mother can use her own furniture when she moves into Westbury Center. Didn't you tell me you put your family things in storage in Raleigh?"

"That's wonderful. She'll love having her own things even if she only remembers them once in a while." This was all just too damn coincidental or she was becoming paranoid. On the way to North Carolina to pick up her mother, she'd stopped at the storage unit she'd paid rent on all these years and hid the pillowcase with the bank money in one of the dresser drawers, keeping ten thousand dollars in case of an emergency. She'd replaced the two hundred dollars from her own account and then taken ten thousand. What kind of pretzel logic was that? A criminal mentality was taking over her mind, and there wasn't anything she could do about it.

"Mom really likes those ladies that are staying with her, doesn't she?" Annie said to have something to say.

"She calls them both Grace. They don't mind, though. They understand. Helen likes me. A lot," Elmo said slyly.

Annie and Jane whooped with glee. Elmo's face turned fire red. "When is your house going to be ready?"

"Three weeks, and, no, she isn't moving in. Helen, not your mother. I like to play chess, and so does she. She doesn't like tuna and she hates coffee. Drinks tea all day long. Sweet tea, they call it down here. That's all there is to it. Don't you two be badgering me now."

"A nifty bachelor like yourself is going to find himself in big demand around here. Before you know it you'll be beating off all those rich widows with a stick. They're going to try and tempt you with their shrimp and grits and their she crab stew," Annie teased.

"Hrumph. Don't like grits and never did care for stew. I'll be seeing you in a bit. Be sure to lock up tight."

"We will. Dinner's at eight."

"I'll be there."

"If you don't need me, then I'm off, too," Jane said.

"Go ahead. I have to do the books. I'll be home by eight."

"Annie, we're doing so well, it's scary. If we wanted to, we could buy ourselves a new outfit. When was the last time we did that?"

"At least a hundred years ago. We need a fella before we get duded up."

"I'm looking." Jane laughed as she scooted for the front door.

* * *

Annie brushed at a swarm of gnats as she made her way down the street. The humidity made it hard to breathe. Her mind wandered as she passed tourists and summer-school students. Where had the time gone? It seemed like yesterday that they opened the Daisy Shop, and here it was mid August. In another week the fall-term students would be swarming back onto the campus and they'd be run ragged again. Still, it was always better to be busy. When you were busy you didn't have time to think. Some days she almost forgot about her big, dark secret. As Jane said a while back, things were going so well it was downright scary.

Her mother loved the Westbury Center, where she now lived. She worked in her garden every day, played the piano on occasion, and actually seemed to have a routine of sorts. She cooked simple things, and if she forgot to wash the dishes, there was someone to do it for her. She had adopted a kitten from the petting zoo and walked it on a bright blue leash several times a week. Visitor days were happy occasions. Jane and Elmo always went with Annie, and, weather permitting, they picnicked in the small walled garden.

Norma Jean Clark was happy. Annie was grateful.

"Oh, I'm terribly sorry. I wasn't watching where I was going. I guess I was woolgathering."

"Now that's an expression I haven't heard in years. My grandmother used to say that. It wasn't your fault, it was mine. Daniel Matthew Evans," the man said by way of introduction.

Annie laughed. "Anna Daisy Clark," she said, holding out her hand.

"I don't think I ever met anyone named Daisy. You wouldn't by any chance be the Daisy from the Daisy Shop, would you?"

"I am indeed."

"Best coffee I ever drank. I like those tuna sandwiches, too."

"I don't think I ever saw you in the shop," Annie said.

"Usually I have one of my students pick it up for me. I'll have to make it a point to come by more often."

Annie laughed again. *My God, I'm flirting.* "We have a pretty good brownie on Mondays. Goes with the sandwich, no extra charge. Mondays are downers as a rule. Does that make sense?"

"In a cockamamie kind of way."

"You don't look like a professor," Annie blurted. She felt her neck grow warm. "I'm sorry, I didn't mean to say that."

"Of course you did. Don't apologize. My mother doesn't think I look like a professor, either. It's these shorts and running sneakers. Now you, on the other hand, look like both a Daisy and an Annie."

"I'll take that as a compliment."

"It was meant as one. See you around. I have three more miles to go. It was nice meeting you, Anna Daisy Clark."

"Likewise," Annie called over her shoulder. Wait until she told Jane about this encounter. She practically danced the rest of the way home.

Ten minutes later, Annie bounded up the steps and into the apartment, yelling at the top of her lungs. "Jane, you aren't going to believe this. I just met this man. I think he's a professor. Jane, where the hell are you? I think he was gorgeous, but I can't be sure. It was dark. I bumped into him. Talk about chance happenings. He had great legs and nice buns. Do we have any wine. It's in our budget this week, isn't it? Oh, I didn't know you had company. I'm sorry. I could go back out and come back in like a lady instead of a hooligan." Her eyes full of questions, Annie waited for an introduction.

"Annie, this is Peter Newman. He's investigating the bank robbery in Boston."

"Really. How can we help you, Mr. Newman?" Annie said, sitting down across the table from him. "You came all the way to South Carolina to talk to us. No wonder insurance rates are so high. Do we have wine, Jane? Maybe Mr. Newman would like some.'' *I can pull this off. I know I can do this. Stay calm and cool. There's no evidence. Take it slow and easy. The ten thousand dollars is safe in your dehumidifier. He'd never look there. Besides, he needs a warrant before he can search the house. Cool and calm. I can do this.*

"Mr. Newman said he ran our license plates," Jane said coolly.

"Why?" Annie asked as she sipped the wine Jane handed her. *He looks like a skinny bulldog,* she thought.

"It wasn't just your cars. We ran the plates from all the cars parked in the campus parking lot. Those that we could make out. The rest we got from the campus parking authority. We're talking to everyone."

"What do you want to know?"

"Where were you when the robbery occurred?"

"I was in the drugstore buying aspirin. I walked because it was such a beautiful day. I was talking to Mr. Richardson, or maybe I was paying him. I'm not sure. We both heard the shot at the same time. When I was walking home, I crossed the lot and saw what happened. That's all I know."

"I was in our apartment," Jane said. "Actually, I was getting ready to go to the post office to drop off our change of address when Annie came in. In the excitement of worrying about my money in the bank, I forgot to go. I never did leave an address."

"Did either one of you see or hear anything else?"

Both women shook their heads.

"Do you always leave your car windows open?"

"The backseat windows of my car really stick. If it's nice out, I let them down. If it's raining, I struggle with them. But, to answer your question, most of the time in nice weather they're down," Annie said

"Mine too. I'm just too lazy to roll them up," Jane said. "Why?"

"We think there's a possibility the robber tossed the money bag into one of the cars on the campus lot."

"But I thought the robber gave the money to a third person," Annie said, her eyes wide and innocent.

"We haven't ruled out that possibility."

"Almost all the cars on campus have their windows open in the spring," Jane said. "There was a picture in the morning paper on graduation day. I saw the picture on the front page and almost all of them had the windows open. Are you saying you suspect *us?*"

"I'm not saying that at all."

"Then what are you saying?" Annie asked bluntly.

"I'm saying we're at the asking-questions stage."

"Maybe you should post a reward," Jane said. "They do that on television shows all the time."

Annie held her glass out for a refill. Jane poured for Annie and herself, a worried look on her face. "Is there anything else you want to ask us?"

"Not at this time. I might have questions later on."

"Then it might be a good idea to call ahead," Annie said.

"Why is that?"

"Because you're eating into our dinner hour. As you can see it's almost eight o'clock. We get up at five. It's been a long, hard day, and I want to relax before I go to bed and have to get up and do it all over again. In short, Mr. Newman, I'm dog-ass tired. If there's nothing else, I'd like to eat my dinner."

"Then I'll be on my way. I'm sorry for the inconvenience. I'm just doing my job. If you give me your phone number, I will call ahead."

It's just a formality. It doesn't mean anything. Be cool. Look him in the eye. Annie got up from the table and reached into the cabinet for the dinner plates as Jane handed over a slip of paper with their phone number on it.

"The number on the bottom is the Daisy Shop. We're there all day long and don't have an answering machine," Jane said.

"Nice little shop. I saw it earlier."

"We started it with less than five hundred dollars and a lot of hard work," Annie snapped irritably.

"That's what Mr. Peabody said. Good night, ladies."

I'm going to faint or throw up or both and choke at the same time, Annie thought. She swigged from the wineglass until her eyes started to water.

"Do you think he suspects *us?*" Jane asked nervously. "By the way, Elmo canceled. The lovely Helen is preparing something for him."

"Us? Nah. He was just being obnoxious. Was he a detective or an insurance person?"

"Both I think. Investigative insurance adjuster. Something like that. He reminded me of a bulldog. Smart-ass."

Annie forced a laugh. "Hey, he can go through my car anytime he wants."

"I think he did. Mine too."

"He needs a warrant," Annie said.

"Maybe he just stood outside and looked in or something. Guess what, my windows are down."

Annie's laugh was genuine this time. "So are mine. So are half the car windows in this city. So, what's for dinner? Boy, I can't wait to tell you about this guy I bumped into. We are talking hand-some!"

"Since Elmo canceled, I decided on filled peppers, and tell me more."

"There he was in those cute running shorts . . ."

It was close to midnight when Annie pulled her diary out of her knitting bag. *I met two men today. My heart feels like it's too big for my chest and will explode any minute. I feel frightened and yet I feel elated. A lady from Texas bought three of Jane's paintings today. Business has quadrupled.*

* * *

Annie looked at the calendar on the small makeshift desk in the back room. Time to pay the quarterly taxes. Her eyes crossed when she stared at the neat rows of numbers in the ledger. "We need an accountant. All this stuff is eating into my time," she grumbled to Jane. "Elmo is like a caged cat. He says we need to open another shop over by the Baptist College in North Charleston. How are we going to do it, Jane, and keep up with all this?"

"We have to delegate. One of us needs to be here all the time. So far we've been lucky with the two part-timers we hired. I guess we do need to hire more help. Elmo has a very good business head, but he's running us ragged."

"I know," Annie said. "He's right, though. It is time to open another shop. We can afford it as long as we don't go overboard. God, Jane, do you remember how we had those ten coffeepots from Super Mart when we first opened? Twelve cups to a pot and all ten of them were going all day long. That fancy-dancy Bunn coffeemaker is a godsend. I can't wait till we have enough money to buy the cappuccino machine. This is just so fantastic."

"See, Annie, our gut instincts were right. We're making more money serving coffee than we would make working in the business world. I get to paint, drink all the coffee I want, and know I'm a half owner in a business that is thriving. What more could anyone want?"

"More hours in the day. A day off just to sleep once in a while. A couple of really nice men in our lives. I'd settle for all of the above." Annie laughed.

"Speaking of men. What's with the professor?"

"He's called for dates three times and three times he canceled. I gave up on him. Now, are you in favor of hiring an accounting firm to handle all of this?"

"Absolutely. I'll check it out today. I'm ahead on my post-cards. I can paint them now with my eyes closed. Some man came in here last week and said he would hang some of my pictures in his gallery on Charlotte Street. He said I just might be the next Josie Edell. I don't know who she is, but he sounded impressed."

"Oh, Jane, that's wonderful. Then it's settled. You're going to find us an accounting firm. I'm going to go over to the college and post a notice for more part-time help, then I'm going to head out to the Baptist College and check out the situation."

"As long as you're going over to the college, why don't you take the professor some coffee and brownies?" Jane asked slyly.

"Why don't you mind your own business." Annie grinned.

"Phone's ringing," Jane said.

"The phone's always ringing. You get it."

"You're closer," Jane shot back.

"Daisy Shop," Annie said, a smile in her voice.

"Miss Clark, or is it Miss Abbott?"

"This is Annie Clark. How can I help you?"

"This is Peter Newman."

Annie's voice soured immediately. "What can I do for you, Mr. Newman?"

"You can give me permission to run a forensics test on yours and Miss Abbott's automobiles. We're checking all the cars. There's a possibility fibers from the canvas money bag might show up. We're now working on a theory that the money bag was tossed into one of the cars with open windows and then a third party retrieved it later on."

"That's going to be difficult, Mr. Newman. My car gave out on me about three weeks ago, so I junked it. I can give you the name of the scrap dealer. Jane's car is still here if you want to check it."

"When would be a convenient time?"

"I'll put Jane on the phone. You'll have to work out a time with her. The junk dealer is Casey and Sons in Jedburg."

Annie made a face as she handed the phone to Jane. She turned away to gather up the papers on her desk, her heart pounding so loud she thought for sure Jane would hear it.

Jane slammed down the phone so hard it bounced out of the cradle. "That damn guy just doesn't give up. Fibers my foot! Do you think he's harassing us? He's coming by at six on Wednesday. My, God, Annie, what if it was my car? What if there are fibers in it?"

"Jane, you didn't do anything wrong. If somebody dumped something in your car and took it out later, you are not responsible."

"Tell that to some cop when he comes to arrest us. I could tell by the look on his face that night he came to the apartment that he didn't believe one thing we told him. He thinks there's something fishy about us. The suspicion just oozed out of his pores."

"He's doing his job. He's leaving no stone unturned. Isn't that what they say on those cop shows on television?"

"Yeah. What'd that junk guy say he was going to do with your old bus?"

"Sell it for parts and compact the frame. It's probably in some landfill by now."

"That guy will buy hip boots and go digging around. Trust me."

"Do you think so?"

"Yeah, I think so. He's probably thinking you did it on purpose to get rid of the evidence. I bet the rat is calling the scrap dealer as we speak."

Annie's heart skipped a beat. "So let him." Her voice was so defiant-sounding, Jane raised her eyebrows. "I think the guy is a weasel, and I didn't like him the first time I met him. He's slick. If he bothers us again, I think we need to report him to his agency.''

"I'll be glad to do it.''

"Ha! You'll have to fight me for the phone. Nothing would give me greater pleasure.''

"I'm going to try and find a female CPA. I'll be back in a little while. Are you sure this is all I need to give him or her.''

"It better be. It's all I have. Good luck, Jane.''

Annie sat for a long time, one hand on top of the phone. Should she call Casey and Sons or leave well enough alone? Leave well enough alone. If a car was compacted, would it be possible to pry it open? Could the old mats and seats be taken out? Did Casey and Sons sell the seats or the mats? Was the insurance investigator trying to scare them? If he was, he was doing a good job.

She was scared out of her wits.

CHAPTER FOUR

Annie sat alone in the living room of her new house staring at the twinkling Christmas tree lights. With the two Daisy Shops closed for holiday break, she felt at loose ends. Two days of sleeping around the clock had left her rested ... and bored. These days Elmo was busy with his two lady friends, Jane was dating the accountant who was managing their financial records, and her mother was so busy at Westbury Center she didn't want to be bothered with visits from her daughter.

She toyed with the idea of calling Daniel Matthew Evans but realized at the last moment that he, too, like his students, probably went home for the holidays. One luncheon date and one concert hardly made for a relationship or gave her the right to call and ask him to come over for a glass of wine.

She felt tense and didn't like the feeling. Was something going to happen? All manner of horrible thoughts whirled through her head. Was the bulldog going to show up and ruin their holidays? Was Elmo going to get sick? She worried about him. Would Jane get serious with Bob Granger? Three dates a week and all-day weekends led her to believe so. She was happy for Jane, but just a tad jealous.

Damn! What is wrong with me? Maybe I should call Tom. She hadn't spoken to him since early summer. The holidays were a time for forgiveness and family. It wouldn't hurt her to call him just to wish him and the kids a happy holiday. She'd sent gifts and even included one for Mona. It wouldn't have hurt him to call and say thank you. Maybe he was embarrassed. Maybe a lot of things.

Annie bounded up from the couch and started to pace. She liked this new house of hers. It was old, ancient really, but it had character and great old fireplaces and wonderful heart-of-pine floors. The furniture was sparse but sufficient for now. Later, when she had more time, she would pick and choose furniture that would go with the old antebellum house. It still boggled her mind that she owned a house at all. Like Elmo said, "You need the tax deduction now."

Annie poured herself a glass of wine as she continued to pace. Without realizing it, she was on the second floor, her hand on the closet doorknob. The dehumidifier box with the ten thousand dollars was still there, pushed to the end of the long shelf. The same money she'd used to set her mother up at Westbury. She should have given it back a long time ago. The ideal time would have been when Newman tried to track down her old car with no results. Why was she keeping it? Was she afraid to give it back? Was it some kind of security? What did she hope to gain from keeping it? Nothing. Absolutely nothing.

Annie closed the louvered doors to the closet. Her head was above water. She was able to pay for her mother's care, she'd bought this house and a secondhand car that looked good and ran like a dream. Nothing extravagant, just a good, serviceable car. The interest payments were deductible along with her mortgage interest as well as the monies she paid out for her mother's care. All her bills were paid, and she had money in the bank—not a lot but enough of a cushion to make her feel comfortable. Right now she and Jane could sell the Daisy Shops for a handsome profit if she wanted to. Her heartbeat quickened when she thought of the two new shops that were going to open up after the first of the year, both of them at Clemson University. "A veritable gold mine," Elmo had chortled. And he was right. Elmo was always right. He was probably right about the business plan he'd hired someone to draft up, too. She wasn't sure about the plan to hire a business manager, though. Someone to handle the accounting was different. No one was going to handle her money but Jane and herself.

The phone rang just as Annie poured herself a second glass of wine—or was it her third? She looked at the small clock on the mantel: 10:15. An hour and fifteen minutes past her normal bedtime. Her greeting was cautious. It might be Newman, with some new trick up his sleeve.

"Annie, it's Tom. The kids told me you sent them some Christmas presents. I'm calling to thank you and to ask you how Mom is. Look, Annie, if you don't want to talk to me, it's okay."

"I have mixed feelings, Tom. I sent a gift for you, too."

"I was sure you did. I guess Mona didn't see fit to give it to me. I haven't been to the house in quite a while."

"What does that mean, Tom?"

"It means Mona and I separated in September. I'm living in a small apartment. It's hard as hell paying support and trying to maintain a life for myself. She's going to clean me out. That's not really why I called. I wanted to ask about Mom and to tell you some guy was here asking questions about you and Jane. I told him off, then booted his ass out the door. I'd had a couple of beers, but he gave me the impression he thinks you, Jane, and that guy you worked for are somehow involved in some bank heist. I could be wrong about this, but Mandy said he came to the house and talked to Mona. Christ alone knows what the hell she would say. I just thought you should know. I'm not even going to ask you about that because I know what kind of sterling character you are and the guy was so full of it his eyes were turning brown. How's Mom?''

Annie's heart hammered in her chest. ''Mom's doing great, Tom. She really seems happy. Most times when I go to see her she doesn't want to visit. She has friends and she gardens. The little villa she has is just perfect for her. She doesn't wander off, and the security is great. She's coming for Christmas. I have a real tree and everything. We closed up shop, since the college is closed. So is Bishop England. What are you doing for Christmas, Tom?''

''I'll probably sleep all day. Mona took the kids kicking and screaming to her parents' house.''

''Why don't you come here? I have an extra bedroom, and I know Mom would love to see you. It's been a long time since you've seen her.''

''I can't afford it, Annie. I don't have two extra nickels to rub together. It's kind of you to ask since I . . .''

''Will you come if I get you a ticket?''

''You don't have to do that, Annie. Drink a toast to me. I don't want you feeling sorry for me.''

''I don't feel sorry for you. You're my brother. I'd love it if we could all spend Christmas together. Say yes, Tom. I'll call the airline and make the reservation now and you can take the next flight. I'll pick you up at the airport. It will be like old times.''

''Okay, it's a deal. Listen, Annie, you and Jane aren't in any kind of trouble, are you?''

''No, of course not. That guy has been dogging us for months now. Sooner or later, he'll give up. If he doesn't stop soon, though, I'm going to call his home office and tell them he's harassing us. Elmo is getting real feisty about all of this. I think because he sold his drugstore and moved here when we did, the investigator thinks we had something to do with it. The shops are doing extremely well. He's probably running bank checks on us and all that other stuff they manage to do. Whoever would have thought he would track you down in California? Hang up, Tom, and I'll call the airline and then call you back."

"I'll pack in the meantime. Jeez, Annie, this is so nice of you."

"If you could, would you do it for me?"

"Yeah, Annie, I would. I want you to believe that."

"Okay, then. Hang up."

The moment Annie hung up the phone, she dropped her head to rest between her legs to ward off the dizziness engulfing her. *I have to give it back. I have to give it back. I'm sending it back. I'm sending it back as soon as I can figure out a way to do it without it coming back to haunt me. I'm going to do it. I swear I am. I can't take this anymore. Get a grip, Annie. It's all part of the investigative process. If he does suspect, this is his way of trying to wear you down. If you send it back now, he'll know it was you. You replaced all the money you borrowed. You're just holding it for the right time to mail it back.*

Annie gave her head a shake to clear her thoughts before she dialed the airline. Within minutes she had a reservation for her brother on the red-eye. She whipped her credit card out of the desk drawer and rattled off the numbers. It was the first time she'd used the card since coming to South Carolina. It gave her a good feeling to know she could afford to charge the ticket and pay it off when the bill came in. A very good feeling. "Do what you want with this, Mr. Snoop," she muttered. There was no doubt in her mind that the insurance investigator had her account as well as Jane's flagged for any charges that might appear. "Tough, Mr. Snoop. Just plain old tough.

"You know something else, Mr. Snoop?" Annie said, sloshing more wine into her glass. "I'm going to be so successful you aren't going to believe it. I'm going to do it on my own, too. By the time I'm thirty I'm going to be a millionaire.''

As she guzzled the wine, her head spinning, Annie placed the call to her brother. "It's all set. Just go to the airport and take the United red-eye. I'll pick you up in the morning. I'm glad you're coming, Tom.''

"Are you okay, Annie? You sound like you've been crying.''

"Actually, Tom, I'm probably drunk. I'm not sure why that is. Then again, maybe I do know, and I just don't want to deal with it.''

"Are you by yourself, Annie?''

"Yes. I bought this beautiful old house, but I don't have much furniture. I do have a Christmas tree. Jane is seeing someone. We don't see too much of each other after work anymore. Elmo is fending off two ladies who are hot on his tail, and he loves every minute of it.''

"Guess you're feeling kind of shortchanged, huh?''

"Kind of. All I do is work. I did meet a professor, but he canceled out on three different dates, so yeah, I'm alone. I might get some goldfish. Remember when we had gerbils, Tom?''

"Yeah, one day we had one and the next day we had twenty-three or was that hamsters?''

"Who cares. We had them. Ya know, Tom, sometimes Mom has a spark and she remembers me. Then I cry and blow the whole moment. I hope she remembers you.''

Tom's voice was husky. "Yeah, let's hope so. Can I bring you anything from sunny California?''

"I thought you said you didn't have any money.''

"I don't, but I still have a charge card. Name it.''

"Just yourself, Tom. We can go shopping when you get here and buy Mom some stuff for Christmas. Remember how she always loved the wrappings better than the presents. What'd you do with the money from the sale of the house, Tom?''

"Paid Dad's medical bills. There were two mortgages. I paid those off. Mom's condition hit around then. More medical bills. I have all the records, Annie. I would never snow you on that."

"I never liked your shitty wife," Annie said, uncorking a second bottle of wine. "You were too good for her. I like your kids, though. Do you think I'll ever have kids, Tom?"

"Not at the rate you're going. We'll have to do something about that."

"Yes, let's do something about that. Somebody without any deep, dark secrets. I hate people who have secrets."

"Are you trying in your own inimitable way to tell me *you* have a deep, dark secret?"

"Me? Sorry. No secrets here. Do you have any?"

"I was going to keep my divorce from you, so I guess I don't, now that I told you. You probably should go to bed, Annie."

"Why is that, Tom?"

"So you're bright-eyed and bushy-tailed when it's time to pick me up instead of being hungover. Is that a good enough reason?"

"The best," Annie hiccuped. "What's it like to be really happy, Tom?"

"How about if I tell you tomorrow when you pick me up. Unplug your tree lights and go to bed. Will you promise me to do that?"

"Sure, Tom."

"Good girl. I'll say good night then."

Annie corked the wine bottle and dutifully turned off the Christmas tree lights. She thought about her old cat Flossie as she made her way up the stairs to her bedroom. It had always been her job to let the cat out before going to bed.

Tomorrow she was definitely going to get some goldfish.

*   *   *

Annie waited impatiently, her head throbbing, for her brother to walk through the gate. When she saw him she ran, her arms outstretched. "I'm so glad you came, Tom. This is going to be such a good Christmas. I'm going to cook a big turkey with all the trimmings. Do you have baggage?"

"A ton of it and something special for you. I took vacation time."

"That's great. How long?"

"Do you think you can put up with me for a whole month? I thought maybe I could help out a little. I owe you, Annie."

"I can use all the help I can get if you're serious. I can even offer you a job if you want one. We're going to open two shops near the Clemson campus. I'd love to turn one over to you. Both actually. You won't be making what you made in California, but the cost of living here is less. We're going big-time here. That means health benefits, a profit-sharing plan, all the coffee and tuna you want."

"I'll take it."

"Really, Tom?"

"Really, Annie."

"What about the kids?"

"Mona is playing hardball. She wants alimony and astronomical child support. I might as well tell you, she has a boyfriend. That's what started the whole thing. But, to answer your question about the kids, you'll have to give me time off to visit them or to fly them here. My lawyer says I can get them summers, weekends, and some holidays. Once every six weeks sounds good to me with the holidays and summers."

"That would be so nice, Tom. Which bags are yours?"

"The two big gray ones. They have wheels. We can't go yet. I have to wait for your present to come up. Stay here with the bags. I think I see it now."

Annie craned her neck to see where her brother was going, but the heavy holiday traffic pushed and jostled her until she finally gave up. It would be like Tom to bring her an orange tree loaded with oranges. She sat down on top of the largest traveling bag to wait. When she felt a tap on her shoulder she turned.

"Merry Christmas, Annie," Tom said, handing her a bright blue dog kennel.

"A dog! You got me a dog! Oh, Tom, how wonderful! Can I take him out? What's his name?"

"Of course you can take him out. He's yours. Rosie is her name. She's the best of the best, Annie. Championship lines all the way. Now that you're living alone, you need someone like Rosie here."

"A German shepherd! Oh, she's just gorgeous. I love her. I will love her forever and ever. Oh, Tom, this is just so wonderful of you." Annie buried her face in the dog's soft fur. She thought she could hear the dog purr her approval.

"You have to bond with her. That means you hold her close to your heart and snuggle with her. I didn't handle her at all because I didn't want to confuse her. Tell me where the car is, and I'll get it. You stay here with the baggage and Princess Rosie. She's six weeks and two days old. Do you really like her, Annie? You know, really like her?"

"How could I not, Tom. She's adorable."

"You can do anything you want. She's your dog. Now, where's the car?"

"It's a Volvo station wagon. Dark green and parked in Row C, third one from the end. Here's the key. Drag the bags outside, and I'll carry the kennel. We'll wait on the curb for you. Oh, look, she's asleep."

"She can feel your heart beat so she feels safe with you," Tom said.

"How'd you learn so much about dogs? We always had cats."

"I got a crash course last night. I found this dog in a little less than three hours and still made it to the airport. I have *books* in my baggage on what to do and not do. The breeder said you need to read them. All of them," he said ominously.

"Okay," Annie said, nuzzling the dog. This time she thought she heard the puppy sigh. Suddenly her world felt right side up. Tom was here and bygones would now be bygones. She wouldn't be alone anymore, and now she would have someone to love. Someone to love her back. "You can't take Mom's place but you'll do," she whispered into the puppy's ear. "This is going to be the best Christmas ever."

Annie set the table as the new pup tweaked her ankles and shoes. She was everywhere, but always within sight, curious and devilish as she explored every inch of the old house.

"Okay, big gal, let's go for a stroll in the garden. We don't want any messes when company gets here. Go get your leash. That's a good girl," Annie praised, as Rosie brought her a frayed and tattered string that had once been a leash. "Guess it's a chain from now on. We do not chew our leashes. Is that understood?"

The shepherd sat up on her haunches, her ears straight as arrows as she stared at her mistress. Her bark was deep and joyful at the prospect of an outing.

Annie walked the dog through the garden. "You know, Rosie, I bought this house because of the garden. I saw myself sitting out here on one of those old Charleston rockers, reading and sipping lemonade. I bet that angel oak is at least three hundred years old if it's a day. When you get a little bigger you're going to love lying under it. It stays green all year long, so on sunny days we can come out here to contemplate the conditions of the world and my deep, dark secret that suddenly doesn't seem so deep and dark. Of course that just means I'm in denial.''

Annie eyed the ancient wooden gate with the stout padlock. No one could get in from the outside. If she wanted to, she could hide out here for days, and no one would know the difference. She watched indulgently as Rosie dug at the luscious green moss growing between the cobbled stones. She didn't stop her. It was, after all, her garden, too. She'd outgrow her curiosity soon enough. She stopped her frantic pawing, her puppy eyes alert, her head tilted to the side. "Company, huh? Yes, I hear the car. Okay, let's go in and welcome our guests.''

The little dog bounded across the small courtyard to struggle up the two steps that led to the kitchen. Annie had to boost her fat little bottom over the second hurdle. She woofed her pleasure when Tom walked into the kitchen, Norma behind him. The pup sniffed his shoes and growled as she pawed at Norma's leg. Tom scooped her up into his arms, and said, ''You should have warned me, Annie. You did, but I still wasn't prepared. There hasn't been one sign of recognition.''

''I know. It's like that sometimes, then bingo, she'll say something that makes perfect sense.''

''Mom, I'm so glad you could come. Isn't it wonderful that we're all going to spend Christmas together?''

''Did we get a tree? I don't seem to remember that. What's your name again? This nice gentleman didn't introduce us.''

''Anna Daisy Clark, Mom. Are you hungry? I made a turkey and all the stuff you used to make on holidays. I can give you some to take back when you leave.''

''That would be nice. This isn't my house. My kitchen cabinets are white with those little crisscross panes. Who lives here?''

''Me and Tom. Would you like a glass of wine, Mom?''

''If this is Christmas, then I'd like a good slug of bourbon.

Did anyone see my husband? We always had bourbon on Christmas. Never mind, he's probably shoveling the snow. We'll have it later. I keep forgetting I need to mind my p's and q's. I didn't say anything wrong, did I?''

"No, Mom." Annie met her brother's gaze and muttered, "I'll explain it all later."

"More company," Tom said. "I'll get it." Still carrying the dog, he pushed his way through the swinging door.

"He's such a nice man. He reminds me of someone," Norma said vaguely.

"Tom's your son, Mom. I'm Annie, your daughter. Don't you remember?"

"I remember your secret. I didn't tell anyone. I really didn't."

Annie stared into her mother's eyes and swore later that she felt her blood run cold. "We promised not to mention it, Mom. I didn't tell anyone about your secret. Please don't mention it again."

"All right, my dear. I like your name."

"Lazy Daisy. That's what you used to call me."

"Yes. I forget sometimes. It smells wonderful. The owner must be a good cook."

"She is. She had the best teacher in the world," Annie said, biting down on her lower lip. "Let's go into the living room. We have company. We need to be sociable."

"That's what Joe always says. Where in the dickens is that man? Did it snow that much?"

"I guess so. Mom, do you remember Jane and Elmo?"

"No. Maybe Joe remembers who they are. I haven't seen Flossie for a while. Did she get out?"

"I think she's upstairs," Tom said.

"Oh."

"Listen up everyone," Jane said, her face flushed. "Bob and I have an announcement to make."

I knew it. I knew it, Annie thought as her stomach started to churn.

"Bob asked me to marry him. Look," she said, flashing her new engagement ring.

"Oh, Jane, I'm so happy for you both. When's the big day?"

"Valentine's Day. Isn't that romantic? Annie, Bob wants to move to San Francisco. A friend offered him a partnership in a four-man firm. I'll be able to paint all day long. I know you're upset. Please don't be. Bob can still do your accounting. It won't be a problem."

"Jane, I can't buy you out."

"Oh, Annie, I'm not asking you to buy me out. I'm giving the shops to you. You really did all the work. It was your idea. I just helped. You don't owe me anything."

"No, no, that's not fair. You worked as hard as I did to get them up and running. I could never do that, and you know it."

"Okay, how about this then? Someday when you're a multimillionaire, you give me one of the shops. If you don't like that idea, it's okay with me. Honestly, Annie, I don't want anything. I feel terrible leaving you like this. But, now that your brother is here, I don't feel so bad."

"It sounds like a good deal to me," Norma chirped.

"Do you think so, Mom?"

"Your brother is so handsome, isn't he, Annie?"

"The handsomest guy I know," Annie said in a choked voice. She watched as Tom wrapped his mother in his arms, his eyes glistening with unshed tears.

"That's because I get my looks from you," he said gruffly.

Rosie growled playfully as one paw snaked out to play with the string of pearls around Norma's neck. Annie smiled when her mother giggled at the dog's antics. "Tom and I will take anything we can get," she murmured. Only Tom heard her and nodded his agreement.

"Annie, are you okay with this?" Jane asked.

"Of course I am. I would never stand in your way. I don't want you to give it all up, though. If you're sure one shop for you is okay, then it's okay with me. Consider it a nest egg for the future. It's expensive to put kids through college even on a partner's pay. I'll find a lawyer after the first of the year to draw up the papers. We want to do this all legal. I'm happy for you, Jane, I really am. This is turning out to be a wonderful Christmas. I wonder where Elmo is?"

"There's the doorbell. Right on time. Is he bringing either one of his lady friends?" Jane asked.

"Nope. He said he wanted to enjoy Christmas Eve with his family. Is he going to give you away at your wedding?"

"You bet!" Jane said. "I want you to be my maid of honor. We're just going to do the JP thing. We'll do dinner, then be on our way to San Francisco."

"I'm so jealous," Annie said.

"It's not your time yet, child. The right man will find you when it's time."

"Is that a promise, Mom?"

"Lazy Daisy, of course it's a promise. I never broke a promise to you or Tom, did I?"

"No, Mom. Never ever."

Tom beamed.

"Merry Christmas. Merry Christmas," Elmo called out.

"Tell Elmo the news, Jane," Annie said, her eyes star-bright as she put an arm around her mother's shoulders.

"I'm getting married and moving to San Francisco. I want you to give me away. Will you do it, Elmo?"

The wizened little man twinkled. "I'm honored that you would consider me for such an important role. Of course I'll give you away."

"Norma, you're looking particularly pretty this Christmas Eve. And you must be Tom," Elmo said, holding out his hand.

"Seems we're going to have our work cut out for us with Jane leaving us. You up to it, boy?"

"I'm up to it, sir," Tom said, tongue in cheek.

"Then we're in business. It's our job to make Miss Anna Daisy Clark into one of the richest women in the country. I think we can do it. What's your opinion, son?"

"I think we can do it, sir," Tom said, winking at Annie.

"Call me Elmo."

"Where's the bourbon?" Norma queried.

"I'll get it, Mom," Tom said.

When Annie closed and locked the door hours later, she turned to her brother. "All things considered, it was a wonderful Christmas Eve. Mom knew us for a little while. Jane is delirious with happiness. We called your kids, and everyone said 'Merry Christmas.' Elmo is in his glory plotting our next business steps. You're here. I'm here. And I have Rosie. I don't think I could ask for more. Tomorrow we'll go to church, then we'll start working on the new year. Merry Christmas, Tom."

"Merry Christmas, sis," Tom said, wrapping his arms around Annie to hug her until she squealed. Rosie came on the run and skidded to a stop when she saw that it was Tom making her mistress squeal with delight. She backed up a step, squatted, and peed in the middle of the floor, then ran to her kennel, where she went when she made mistakes.

"It's okay, Rosie. My fault. I lost track of time. C'mon, you can come out." The pup waddled her way over to Annie, her tail swishing furiously. Annie scooped her into her arms. "Tomorrow's another day. Let's go to bed, Tom. We can clean up in the morning."

"Sounds good to me. Were you serious about me living here with you, Annie?"

"Yes. I told you, the cost of living here is cheaper. Think of all that extra money you'll have, not having to pay rent in California."

"Elmo has such big plans. Are we up to this, Annie?"

"We're up to it, Tom. Trust me on this. I am going to miss Jane, though."

"You can hire someone to sit at an easel and paint postcards. A young art student will jump at the chance."

Arm in arm, brother and sister walked up the steps.

"I'm glad you're here, Tom."

"Me too, Annie. Thanks for giving me the chance."

"My pleasure. Thanks for giving me this dog. Did I thank you before?"

"At least five hundred times. *That* was my pleasure."

"Night, Tom."

"Night, Annie."

In her room, with Rosie settled on her own little blanket, Annie withdrew the note Jane had passed her early in the evening. Her heart pounded inside her chest when she thought about why her friend hadn't taken her aside to tell her whatever was in the note. Why would Jane write her a note? *She knows.*

Annie sat down on the bed and unfolded the note.

Dear Annie,

I knew tonight would be hectic, and I wouldn't be able to get you alone. Also, I didn't want to spoil the evening. Hence the note. I am so worried about Peter Newman. He's been dogging Bob at the office. I know in my heart of hearts he thinks my car was the one where the money bag was tossed. Maybe by moving to San Francisco, I can get him out of my hair. I don't know why he's homed in on me like he has. He's scaring me and Bob as well. I'm just sorry I don't have your guts when it comes to dealing with that creep. He actually came right out and said I might have had a blanket or something on the floor and then thrown it away. This man is not going to go away. Not ever. I'm just so happy I can't stand the thought of that jerk spoiling my happiness. I haven't had a really good day since that creep invaded our lives, and I know you haven't either, for all your bravado.

Annie, you will always have a special place in my heart, and I want you to be the godmother to my first child. I want us to promise each other we will never let our friendship dwindle away to the point where we just send Christmas cards. You are the sister I never had. The best friend in the whole world. I hope your life turns out to be as wonderful as I hope mine will be.

Much love and affection.

Jane

Annie folded the note and placed it in her night-table drawer. *That does it. The day after Christmas, I'm mailing back the money.* She felt so dizzy and light-headed, she ran to the bathroom and stuck her head under the cold-water faucet. Then she started to cry. *She knows. The note is Jane's way of telling me she knows and would keep the secret. She couldn't face me. She doesn't want to be around me for fear she'll slip and say something or that something will show on her face. I know it as sure as I'm sitting here on this bed.*

If Jane thinks it's me, and Newman thinks it's her, where does that leave me? If I send the money back and Jane moves to San Francisco, will he pursue her? What can he do? He needs proof. He doesn't have proof. The bag went up in flames. The clasp was hacked to pieces and tossed all over the state of North Carolina. He has no proof. Money has fingerprints on it. Well, I can put it in a pillowcase and run it through the wash cycle in the washing machine. I never touched the bearer bonds. I'll wear gloves to pack it up. I can drive to Atlanta and mail it from there. If not Atlanta, then Alabama. Or, I could drive all the way to Virginia or Washington, DC. I'll tell Tom and Elmo I want to scout an area for some new locations.

Then I'll go in the opposite direction. I can do it all in one day. I know I can do it.

If I mail it back and Jane finds out, she'll know for certain her note worked, and it was me all along. Can I live with that?

Maybe I should tell Tom. Tom would know what to do. No, better not to involve anyone. Elmo. God, no.

Annie curled up next to the little dog and hugged her. "We'll think about this tomorrow, Rosie. I'll do the right thing. I really will."

CHAPTER FIVE

Annie waited until she was sure Tom was sound asleep before she crept downstairs with the pillowcase full of money, which she'd been forced to bring home when her mother's furniture was readied for shipment to Westbury Center. Her whole body trembled as she stuffed it into the washing machine in the laundry room. How much soap was required to launder money? Should she use bleach? If she did, would it take the color out of the money? Dear God, what if she ruined it. Maybe she should use vinegar and baking soda. Her mother always said the combination would kill anything in its path. If it could kill an ant pile it should clean the money and destroy any and all of her fingerprints. Which cycle? she dithered. Gentle, normal, heavy-duty, or fine washables? Hot or cold? She started to shake all over again as she turned dials. Hot water and heavy-duty? She set the timer for a fifteen-minute wash cycle. With the soft water here in Charleston, what would she do if the money came out fluffy and hard to manage? "This is insane," she muttered just as the doorbell rang. Who in the world would be ringing her doorbell at ten o'clock on Christmas night?

Annie ran to the door, tripping over her own feet as she went along. She squinted through the peephole and gasped. Daniel.

"Merry Christmas," the professor said, holding out a luscious-looking poinsettia plant and a small gaily wrapped package.

"Daniel! How nice to see you."

Daniel laughed. "Guess I'm a little late. I went to Georgia to see my dad and just got back. I've been gone for the last two weeks."

"Oh."

"A drink would be nice. It is rather cold standing here. If this isn't a good time, I can come back."

"No, no. I'm sorry. My mind has been somewhere else all day. Come in. What would you like to drink?"

"What are you having?"

"Wine."

"Then wine it is. Nice tree. I always chop one down for my dad. We try to pretend it's like past Christmases when Mom was still here and my brothers were around. It never works, but we keep trying. How's your mother?"

"She was here last night. We do that Christmas Eve thing instead of Christmas Day. Mom started it when we gave up on Santa. My brother's here, and she had a few good moments where she knew us."

"Good God, what's that racket?" Daniel asked, whirling around.

"Well . . . it's probably . . . the washing machine probably went off center. I'll just turn it off."

"Let me help you. I'm an old hand where washing machines are concerned. I have this relic in my apartment that goes off center every time I wash a load of clothes. It's really a simple matter of redistributing the load and using your backside to slide the machine back to its original position."

"Really, it isn't a problem. Tom can . . . Tom can adjust it in the morning." She should have given more thought to the contents and going off center. *Damn, why didn't I think of that?*

"It's no problem. For you to be washing on Christmas, the clothing must be important."

"I was bored," Annie said lamely. "See, it stopped all by itself." With all the bouncing around the machine was doing, the money might be shredded by now. *You are one stupid woman, Annie Clark.*

"Tell me, how can you be bored? What are you doing alone on Christmas? Where are all your friends?"

"They're all busy. Elmo is with his two lady friends. Jane is with Bob. They got engaged and are going to move to San Francisco. Tom's here, but he's beat, so he went to bed early. He's going to move here and help with the business. He's going through a divorce."

"Don't tell me any more. Been there, done that. It wasn't a good time in my life. It still isn't. I wanted to tell you, Annie. It's just that I hate talking about it. Right now I can't handle anything more than friendship."

"Friendship is fine. I'm not in a hurry to . . . what I mean is, I'm not ready . . . this isn't coming out right. Friendship is fine. More wine?"

"Sure. That's a pretty tree. Did you have it cut down?"

Annie laughed. "Nineteen ninety-five from the Shell station."

"At least you have a tree. I didn't get one for the apartment. I put up a wreath on the door before I left, and when I got back it was gone. Some kids probably swiped it. I bought mine at the Piggly Wiggly. You know what I always say, if it works, then do it."

"Yeah, I say that a lot myself." Annie giggled. "Listen, if you're hungry, I can make you a turkey sandwich."

"I am, and I'll take it. How about some of that good coffee

of yours? Which brings me to the real reason I came by. When I got to my dad's house a Christmas card was waiting for me from an old college buddy. He owns a coffee plantation in Hawaii. Primo stuff. I called him just for the heck of it and he said you should order your coffee beans direct from him instead of buying through a middleman. Real nice guy. Single, no baggage. Women fall all over him. He's part Hawaiian, part Irish. Great athlete. He whipped my ass at every sport we ever played. He's competitive, rich as sin, and the best friend a guy could have. He was my best man when I got married. Anyway, he'll give you the best deal going. You need to go there and check it out. He said you could stay at the plantation. Trust me when I tell you there's nothing this guy doesn't know about coffee. I think he was weaned on the stuff instead of milk.''

"Really," was all Annie could think of to say.

"Mayo and mustard. Do you have any pickles?''

"I have a whole jar full.''

"You shouldn't have said that. Pickles are my downfall.''

"The only reason I have them is I forgot to put them on the table last night.''

"So you and your brother are going to run the shops, eh?''

"Yes, but we're going to have to hire more help. Do you know any art students who might be interested in sitting in the shop doing the postcards?''

"As a matter of fact, I do. Great kid, hard worker. Gives a hundred percent to anything she does. She paints scenes on sand dollars. That's what's in the present I brought you. I had her come by while I was gone to paint your shop and this house.''

Annie ran into the living room for the small gift box. She oohed and aahed when she saw the sand dollars. "These are beautiful. If she wants the job, tell her it's hers. What about her classes?''

"She clerks at Bob Ellis during the day. Takes classes at

night. She's in the master's program. I'm sure you can work
something out.''

"Full-time. Health benefits. We're working on a profit-
sharing program. It won't be up and running for a while yet.
She helps out behind the counter when it's busy. Base salary,
half of whatever the sand dollars go for. We pay for the paints
and the sand dollars. Sound good?''

"Better than good. She'll take it.''

"How do you know?'' Annie asked curiously.

"Because it beats selling shoes, that's why.'' Daniel laughed.
"If you had a choice, would you like to deal with smelly feet
all day or would you rather sit like a lady and paint sand
dollars?''

"Point well taken. Would you like some pie?''

"I think I'll pass on the pie. I have to pick up my cat Radar
from a friend, and I need some sleep. So, are you going to take
Parker up on his offer?''

"Parker?''

"Parker Grayson. The coffee king.''

"I'll talk to Tom about it in the morning. I'm for anything
that will save me money. We're going to open two shops near
Clemson University. Five hundred pounds of coffee a week is
a lot of coffee.''

"Okay, here's his phone number and address. He said he'd
send someone to the airport to pick you up. All he needs is
two days' notice. I'm outta here, Annie. My eyes are starting
to cross. You're sure now that you don't want me to move
your washer?''

The smile died on Annie's lips. "I'm sure, Daniel. Thanks
for the lovely plant and the sand dollars. What's the girl's
name?''

"Dottie Frances Benton.''

"Tell her to come by and we'll talk.''

At the door, Daniel leaned over and kissed her on the cheek. "Merry Christmas, Annie."

"The same to you, Daniel."

Annie raced out to the laundry room the moment she was certain Daniel was off the porch and headed home. Thank God the laundry room had no windows. In a frenzy, she propped open the top of the washer, to be greeted by a sloppy mess. She tried to lift the pillowcase out of the water, but it was too heavy. Wet money was heavy. In desperation, she tried using two wooden spatulas from the kitchen drawer to try and slide the soggy pillowcase to the center of the washer. Perspiration dripping down her face, she finally managed to push the heavy case full of money to where she thought it would spin more effectively. Her breathing ragged, she turned the dial to the spin cycle. She jumped back when the machine bounded forward but continued to spin. Hardly daring to breathe, Annie waited out the cycle.

"Annie, do you mind telling me what the hell you're doing washing clothes in the middle of the night? What's the machine doing in the middle of the floor?"

"It's okay, Tom. Go back to bed. Rosie threw up on Mom's old quilt, and I decided to wash it. It lumped to the side and made the machine go off center. It's okay, I can handle it." *I'm really getting good at this lying business,* she thought miserably.

"I'm up now, so I might as well help you."

Annie almost choked. "Let's let it go till morning. How about a sandwich?"

"Sure. Do we have any cold beer?"

"Sure we do. I have something to tell you, Tom," she said as she ushered him toward the kitchen. She talked as she sliced turkey onto a plate. "Daniel Evans, that professor I told you about stopped by and brought me these. What do you think?"

"They're pretty."

"They're sand dollars, and one of the students at the college painted them. It's the Daisy Shop and this house. She can take Jane's place if I like her and she wants the job. Basically it would be the same deal I had with Jane.''

Tom chewed with enthusiasm. "This stuff just falls in your lap, doesn't it, sis?''

"Seems that way sometimes. Jane's postcards and her paintings are part of the shop. Kind of like salt and pepper going together. This girl works full-time and goes to school at night. Don't ask me when she studies. Maybe she's a quick learner. Daniel said she sells shoes at Bob Ellis. I'm going to hire her. Do you agree?''

"Of course.''

"He also thinks I should go to Hawaii to talk to his friend Parker Grayson, who has a coffee plantation. He seems to think we can get a better deal on the coffee from him and he might roast it for us, too. Eliminates the middleman. If both shops are successful at Clemson we'll be ordering about five hundred pounds of coffee a week. We need to get the best deal possible.''

"I agree.''

"There's something else, Tom. With Jane and Bob moving to San Francisco, I don't think I want him doing our accounting. I just don't know how to bring it up tactfully without causing hard feelings with Jane. I don't want to have to rely on the mail and worry about will it get there on time. He's been picking up the stuff on a weekly basis. I'm more comfortable with a local firm. What's your feeling?''

"I agree with you on that, too. I can talk to Bob. If it looks like it's getting dicey, I'll say I'm taking it over. Business is business, Annie. When friendship gets involved there's always trouble. I'll be the bad guy and take the hit so your friendship with Jane stays intact. Boy, that was a good sandwich. How about a chunk of that stuffing? Do you remember, Annie, how

Mom always made extra because we liked to eat it cold between two slices of bread? We ate that stuff for weeks.''

"I remember.''

"Do you still write in that diary I gave you on your sixteenth birthday?''

"Every day of my life. All my memories are in there, or as many of them as three lines can hold. Someday when we're both home with the flu or a bad cold, I'll read some of it to you. How come you went to bed so early?''

"I was kind of down. I miss the kids. Seeing Mom and knowing it isn't going to get any better, realizing what a jerk I was where you were concerned. It all kind of piled up on me.''

"There's more, isn't there?''

Tom's face closed up tight. "Yes, but I don't want to talk about it.''

"That's why you should talk about it. Let's have another beer and sit by the tree and talk it out. We used to do that in high school. Then when we went to bed it all seemed bearable.''

"That was a long time ago, Annie. We aren't kids anymore.''

"That's exactly my point, Tom. We're adults now, and we think and act like adults. Now tell me what it is you don't want to talk about.''

"Ah, it's Mona. I don't want my kids having a stepfather. Guys never treat other guy's kids the way they'd treat their own. Ben's immature, and he's sensitive. Jack is mouthy and going through a phase. Mandy is growing up so fast. She wants to be like Mona. Mona is too permissive. I was the disciplinarian. If Mona and the guy she's seeing decide to get married, where does that leave my kids? Even if I lived in California in a house two doors away, Mona would only let me see them on the days the court agreed on. She says I can have them. That's just the way she said it—you can have them if you give me a hundred thousand dollars. Do you believe that! She'd sell her own kids for a hundred grand. I must have been deaf, dumb, *and* stupid when I married her. Even if I had the money, I wouldn't be a part of that. I know Ben heard her that day on the phone when she said it, because he asked me to buy him. I had to do some fast talking to convince the kid he heard wrong.''

"That's terrible, Tom."

"Tell me about it. Right isn't always might as they say. If it's meant to work out, it will. If it isn't, it won't. That's the way I have to look at it. You know, Annie, that's a damn good-looking Christmas tree. What's on our agenda for tomorrow?"

"I think I'm going to go clothes shopping in case I decide to go to Hawaii. You need to meet with Elmo and, if you have the time, take a ride up to Clemson and look it over. Elmo knows the area and will be glad to go with you. Tops, it's a two-hour ride."

"Sounds good. I guess I'll say good night again. I love you, Annie. I really do. If there were times when it didn't seem like I did, I'm sorry. I just had too much on my plate back then."

"I know that, Tom. Sleep tight."

"Where's Rosie?"

"Sleeping on my bed. That long walk before dinner knocked her out. She slept through Daniel's visit."

"That will never happen when she's full-grown. See you in the morning."

"Okay, it's your turn to make breakfast."

"Not a problem."

Annie waited, hardly daring to breathe until she heard Tom's door close, before she beelined to the laundry room. She stared down at the bulging soggy pillowcase full of money. She could buy her niece and nephews from Mona if she wanted to. All she had to do was count out one hundred thousand dollars and hand it over to Tom's soon-to-be-ex-wife, and the kids would be his. There was something so barbaric about the thought she slammed the top of the machine so loud she winced. Then she crossed her fingers that Tom didn't hear the sound. She took a deep breath and held it. When she was satisfied Tom would stay upstairs, she expelled the air in her lungs in a loud *swoosh*.

Using every muscle in her body, Annie struggled with the wet pillowcase until she had it on top of the machine. Her heart pounding with the effort, she managed to get it into the dryer with a loud thump. Huffing and puffing, she turned the knob to high heat and waited to see if the drum would turn. She sighed her relief as the dryer tumbled and turned.

With nothing to occupy her, Annie cleaned the kitchen while she waited for the money to dry. Maybe she should have tried to dry smaller amounts in the microwave. But, to do that, she would have had to handle the money. This way all she had to do was dump the money in a box along with the bearer bonds and mail it back to the bank.

An hour later she cried her frustration when she opened the dryer to find the money almost as wet as when she put it in. She opened the pillowcase to see clumps of bills stuck together. It was obvious that she needed a bigger pillowcase. She turned the dryer back on and sat down on the floor, Indian fashion, to wait, tears dripping down her cheeks. Being a thief wasn't easy.

Three hours later the money was finally dry.

Annie slung the pillowcase over her shoulder and made her way to the second floor, where she tossed it into the closet. She fell into bed and was asleep in minutes, the tears still on her cheeks.

Annie woke slowly, aware of a strange noise in her room. She reached out to touch Rosie, but she was gone. She squinted at the bedside clock: 5:10. It was still dark outside. She switched on the lamp. Rosie bounded onto the bed, a twenty-dollar bill clutched in her teeth. Annie's head felt like it was going to explode right off her neck when she saw the littered money on the floor of the bedroom. Bits and piece of different denominations were everywhere. Her flowered carpet was now a sea of green.

Rosie barked once as she leaned over the side of the bed to inspect her handiwork. Annie gave her a swat as she struggled with the twenty-dollar bill she was planning to chew. It ripped in two. She cursed, using every swear word she'd ever heard her brother Tom use in his hellion days. Any minute now she was going to lose it and have a nervous breakdown.

Annie slid from the bed, her eyes wild with panic. How could she send shredded money back to the bank? On her knees, she tried to gather up the bits and pieces of money to try and determine how much the pup had chewed up. At eight o'clock, with socks on her hands, she counted the money in the pillowcase, finally deciding Rosie had chewed up $23,420. She could send it all back with a note saying . . . what? Did she dare wash the bits and pieces again.

A headache, the likes of which she'd never experienced, thundered inside her head. Rosie bellied over to where she was sitting and crept onto her lap and started to lick her face. She hugged her. The murderous headache subsided almost immediately. "This is a setback. A big one. I'm going to work this out. I know I can work this out. I will work this out."

Rosie leaped off her lap and ran to the door when Tom knocked, and shouted, "Breakfast in ten minutes!"

"Okay. Be right there," Annie responded, her eyes wild. She was a lightning bolt then as she ripped the pillowcase from her pillow. On her hands and knees, she crawled about the room picking up the tattered money. "I know you ate some of this money. I know it. You're going to be pooping twenty-dollar bills all day. If this wasn't so serious, it would be damn funny."

This time, Annie closed the closet door before she bent down to pick up the pup. "Bad dog, Rosie. Now I'm in hock to the bank for more than twenty-three thousand dollars. Oh, well, life is going to go on no matter what I do. I'll find a way to pay it back. I wonder if they'll let Tom bring you to jail when he visits me," she muttered. The pup yipped her pleasure at being carried down the long staircase.

"Oh, it smells good, Tom. What are we having?"

"The works. Pancakes, scrambled eggs, bacon, fresh brewed coffee, and I squeezed the orange juice myself. I know my way around the kitchen. How'd you sleep?"

"I didn't. I had a terrible dream."

"Couldn't be worse than mine. Share." Tom grinned as he filled his sister's plate.

"I dreamed Rosie chewed up twenty thousand dollars I was going to put in the bank," Annie blurted. The moment the words were out of her mouth she wanted to take them back.

"That's not a dream, that's a nightmare. I had this dream that Ben put an ad in a yuppie magazine offering to sell himself to the highest bidder."

"It was the turkey sandwiches and all those pickles we ate before we went to bed," Annie said. "I'm not doing that again."

"Twenty thousand, huh? In your dream did Rosie eat the money or chew it up?"

"Both," Annie said, guilt riding her shoulders like a yoke.

"What'd you do in the dream?"

"I woke up. I don't want to talk about it, Tom. It was a stupid dream. Rosie had been chewing on the newspaper in my room the other day. I guess that's what triggered the whole thing. Great breakfast," she said, pushing her plate away.

"I cooked, so that means you clean up. Get rid of that turkey. I hate eating it for a week after a holiday."

"Bossy, aren't we," Annie said as she got up from the table.

"Just playing big brother, Annie. Twenty thousand? Wow.

Wonder what it means. I'll be in the living room studying Elmo's business plan if you need me.''

Annie wondered why her legs were so shaky. She'd never quite heard that tone in Tom's voice before. Was it her imagination or guilt? She needed a quiet place to think and plan. Maybe she would walk Rosie down to the Daisy Shop, open it up, and sit in the back room and ponder her immediate problem. Yes, that's exactly what she would do.

"I'm taking Rosie for a walk, Tom," Annie called from the kitchen.

"Want some company?" Tom called back.

The last thing she wanted was company. "Nope. It's just me and Rosie."

"Okay, see you later."

"Yeah, much later," Annie muttered as she hooked the leash onto the frisky pup's bright red harness.

CHAPTER SIX

Annie was tired and cranky. It seemed like she'd been traveling for days. Her eyes felt like they were full of grit, and she knew all the moisture had been sucked out of her face. Her hair seemed to have a mind of its own, and her smart linen dress was limp and wrinkled. Her feet and ankles were swollen, and she was getting a headache. If she could have any thing on earth, she would opt for a hot shower and clean hair.

Annie tipped the skycap and looked around for someone who appeared to be looking for her. All she could see were busy travelers in bright-colored garb wearing leis. She felt cheated as well as annoyed that she didn't have one. She'd heard the scent of plumeria was exquisite.

It was hot. Hotter than it was in Charleston when she left. Still, it was the middle of July. Even so, where were the warm, gentle island breezes the brochures touted? Island breezes scented with flowers. All she could smell was diesel fuel and exhaust fumes. "This is not going to endear me to you, Parker Grayson." On the phone, the coffee king had said someone would be waiting for her the moment she got off the plane. "Ha!" she snorted. Two hours later she mumbled, "I'm giving you five more minutes of my time, Mr. Coffee, then I'm outta here. I'll get my coffee from Sumatra. I always wanted to go there anyway."

"Five minutes are up," Annie muttered to no one in particular. Her hand in the air, she hailed a cab. It always paid to have Plan B at one's disposal. "Take me to the nearest hotel, please," she said to the cab driver.

An open-air jeep sailed to the curb the moment the taxi pulled away to enter the steady stream of traffic leaving the Maui Airport. *So much for island hospitality,* she thought sourly as she leaned back in the seat of the cab.

It wasn't just hot, it was sultry hot. The linen dress now felt like a damp dishrag. She winced when she remembered how much she'd paid for it.

"Are you visiting our wonderful island for the first time, miss?" the driver inquired.

"Yes, and it's probably my last."

"Long flight?"

"Very long. I had a four-hour layover in San Francisco. I started out in Charleston, then flew to Atlanta, and from there to St. Louis to San Francisco and from there to your Big Island and then the puddle jumper to here. Someone from the Grayson Plantation was supposed to meet me."

"Their jeep pulled into my parking space when we left. Everyone knows the Grayson jeep. I can turn around and go back if you want me to. I went to school with Roy Alabado. He's the driver. Maybe the jeep broke down or maybe he had a flat. Mr. Grayson is mighty particular about his guests being picked up on time. He treats his guests like royalty."

"The royalty theme doesn't seem to be working today," Annie snapped. "And, no, I don't want to go back."

"I can call Mr. Grayson for you, miss."

"Don't bother. I'll call him myself when I get to the hotel."

"Mr. Grayson usually isn't on Maui at this time of year. He spends most of the year in the Kona district of the Big Island. This is a small island where all the locals know everyone else's business." The driver laughed. "You must be an important guest for Mr. Grayson to come here now."

Annie wasn't impressed or amused. "Do you know Mr. Grayson?"

"We say aloha when we meet. Everyone says aloha to everyone else. It is a custom here in the islands. Mr. Grayson has a fine reputation, and his coffees are sold all over the world. He treats his workers well and all the ladies like him. He's a bachelor with many nieces and nephews on the mainland. He is going to be very upset that you didn't wait for his people to pick you up."

"*He's* going to be upset! Is that what you said? No, no, that's all wrong. I'm the one who is upset. What I should do is buy my damn coffee from the Piggly Wiggly. Oh, we're here. How much is the fare?" Annie counted out money and added a generous tip to offset her surliness, after which she trudged wearily into the hotel, registered, and headed for her room. She showered, washed her hair, turned the air conditioner as high as it would go before she crawled between the crisp, cool sheets. She was almost asleep when she bolted upright to ring the front desk. "Don't put any calls through to my room until I tell you otherwise." A minute later she was sound asleep.

On the ride back to the airport to pick up another fare, the driver stopped to call the airport and have his boyhood friend paged. "This is Miki, Roy. I think I just took your guest to the Royal Hawaiian. That was one pissed off lady. How long you been waiting? Dump the leis and let's catch a beer. Okay, your loss. What do you mean, what should you do? Tell Mr. Grayson you had *two* flat tires. On the other hand, the truth is always an option. Yeah, see you around."

* * *

Golden sunshine found its way into Annie's room just as she opened her eyes. She reached for the small travel clock on the nightstand. Ten minutes past six. She closed her eyes to see if she needed more sleep. When her lids snapped open she dialed room service and ordered breakfast and a newspaper. "No, I do not want to know about my messages. No, I am not interested in any guests sitting in your lobby who are waiting for me. Leave the tray outside the door please." Annie stomped her way to the shower.

Thirty minutes later, Annie opened the door for her breakfast tray. She peeped under the lids. Just as ordered. The paper was folded neatly, there were fresh flowers on the tray, and the coffee smelled heavenly. As she munched and crunched the crisp bacon, she placed a person-to-person call to her brother.

"This was a mistake, Tom," she said the moment she heard her brother's voice. "He left me cooling my heels at the airport for over two hours. He could have paged me. Why is it you guys always stick together? This is not acceptable business behavior. I am calm. I'm eating my breakfast on the balcony and staring at the incredible blue Pacific Ocean. Now I know why they call it a jewel. You want *me* to call *him?* Not in this lifetime, big brother. I'm going to go shopping. Maybe I'll go to the beach and get a sunburn. That's what you're supposed to do when you come to Hawaii. Does Rosie miss me? No kidding. Your whole shoe or part of it? The whole thing? That dog has great teeth. How's business? Ohhh, I like the way that sounds. I have to get dressed. I'll call you tonight. Remember now, there's a five-hour time difference. Don't lecture me, Tom. I think the way I do business has been satisfactory so far. Too bad more people don't operate the way I do. Good-bye, Tom."

At ten minutes past ten, dressed in sandals and a pale blue

sundress, her hair piled high on her head, Annie sashayed down the hall to the elevator. When the door swished open on the ground floor she found herself staring straight into the most incredible blue eyes she'd ever seen in her life. The owner of the blue eyes was also the most handsome man she'd ever seen. She knew exactly who he was.

In the blink of an eye, Anna Daisy Clark fell in love with Parker Grayson. She walked toward him, her eyes appraising him. "Daniel was right. You really do have incredible blue eyes."

He was at her side in an instant, his hand outstretched. Annie clasped it and crunched his hand.

"That's no mean handshake, Miss Clark." Grayson grinned, showing perfectly aligned white teeth that had never seen a set of braces.

"My brother taught me to do it that way. We used to arm wrestle. I always won. You look, Mr. Grayson, like I felt yesterday while I waited for two hours in this blistering heat for a driver who never showed up."

"I apologize. My driver had *two* flat tires. Not just one but two. I've been sitting in this damn lobby since six-thirty last night. That's why I look like this. No matter how you look at it, I'm twelve hours up on you." Annie smiled sweetly. "Is this one of those tit-for-tat things my sisters always talk about? If so, I need to know, so I'll know how to proceed."

In spite of herself, Annie laughed. "I think we're starting out even now." She waited. He was more than handsome, he was—she searched her mind for just the right word—exquisite. Tall, six-three or -four, muscular, perfect tan, amazing dark hair with just a touch of wave or curl. Khaki shorts, deck shoes, and a pristine white shirt. She wondered what their children would look like. "Why are you looking at me like that?"

"Daniel said you were my destiny. I think he might be right. What's your feeling on the subject?" Parker teased lightly.

Her face flushed, Annie said, "I was wondering what our children would look like?"

Grayson's tan turned pink, then red. "If you get your baggage, we should be on our way."

"Then I guess you're going to have to wait a while longer."

"My time is your time, Miss Clark."

"Call me Annie."

"Okay. Annie it is. My mother's name was Anna."

"It's an old-fashioned name. When I was younger I wanted a name like Tiffany or Angelique. When I was sixteen I wanted to change it to Barbarella." Parker laughed as he motioned her to head for the elevator. "Is this where you tell me time is money?"

"Exactly."

Annie jabbed the elevator button. *"Two* flat tires defies belief."

"I knew you would say that. I saw them with my own eyes. The flat tires I mean."

"Really." The elevator swished shut. Annie's closed fist shot in the air. "Yesssss."

"What do you think of my home, Annie?"

Annie looked around, her eyes wide. "It's breathtaking. I don't think I've ever seen anything quite so beautiful. Did you grow up here?"

"Yes. I live on the Big Island most of the year, but I come back for a day or so at a time. I get homesick. My father built the house himself, brick by brick. My mother planted the gardens. The banyan tree that stands sentinel there at the front was the first thing my mother planted after I was born. My mother said my father took one look at the land and knew exactly where to build. It sits on the broad crest of a sloping meadow. If you look you can see the Haleakala Volcano, and if you look down you have a vast view of the North Shore. I surfed there as a youngster. Still do at times with my nephews. They like to take on this old man but invariably they wipe out. I'm still the Big Kahuna as far as they're concerned."

"I never learned to surf," Annie said. "Who tends to the house and all these gorgeous flowers? What is that gorgeous tree?"

"I'll teach you. A couple takes care of it while I'm away. Mattie cooks and cleans while George gardens. That tree is a monkeypod tree. I used to play under it when I was little. My mother read me island stories in the afternoons. I didn't know any other life but this until I was eighteen and went to the mainland to college. I hated being away. I used to count the days until it was time to come home for a holiday or summers, then I fought like a tiger not to go back. To me this is paradise. I don't think there's a prettier place anywhere on earth. I don't know that for a fact. That's what my parents said, and they were world travelers.

"We're within walking distance of freshwater pools and waterfalls. Every afternoon around three o'clock, we have rainbows. Brilliant, perfect rainbows that can be seen for miles. If you like to windsurf, Hookipa Beach is just fifteen minutes away. Five minutes from there is Paia, the Aspen of Hawaii. It's commercial, shopping, excellent restaurants, and a great white-sand beach. Paradise just twenty minutes from the airport. Do you like to wish on the rainbow?"

Annie's heart started to flutter. Just fourteen months ago she'd sat on the floor in her bedroom congratulating herself on the pot of gold at the end of her own personal rainbows. "No. No, I don't. Sometimes you get what you wish for," she said flatly.

Parker laughed. "I know that statement has some deep, dark meaning known only to you. Perhaps you'll share it with me someday." Annie knew the smile on her face looked sickly at

best. "Tell you what. I'll have Mattie fix you a nice cool drink.
You can walk in the gardens or check out the house. It's much
cooler inside. I need to take a shower and change my clothes.
Would you like to freshen up? Mattie will show you to your
room."

"Yes, I think I would."

"Good, I'll see you in a bit then. Mattie, our guest is here,"
he bellowed.

She was incredibly tall and graceful. Ageless with her coronet
of braids and high cheekbones. Her island attire was as regal-
looking as she was. Annie felt like she was in the presence of
royalty. She smiled, and Mattie returned her universal greeting.
"Come, I will show you to your room." Annie followed like
a puppy and then giggled when she saw the woman's bare feet
peeking out from the colorful muu-muu she was wearing.

"Your dress is beautiful," Annie said.

"If you like it, I will make you one. Which color would you
prefer?"

"Oh, no, I didn't mean for you . . ."

"It will be my pleasure. There is not much to do when Parker
isn't here. I sew for his nieces all the time. If you do not have
a color preference, I can make you one that will look like our
daily rainbow. I have many bolts of rainbow silk. You are a
size ten, no?"

"Yes. Size ten." It was an omen of some kind. She was
sure of it. She was jittery now with all the talk of rainbows. *Shift
into neutral,* she cautioned herself. *It's all just a coincidence.*

"I will have your island dress ready when it is time for you
to leave. Freshen up, Miss Clark, and I will have lemonade
ready for you on the lanai."

Annie waited until the door closed before she looked around
at the room that would be hers for the next few days. For some
reason she'd expected white-wicker furniture. Instead she had
wonderful mahogany polished to a high sheen. The floors were

a burnished teakwood. She smiled at the high four-poster, with its colorful spread. A paddle fan circled lazily overhead, while the crisp organdy curtains billowed into the room from the open French doors. She felt almost light-headed with the heady scent of the plumeria wafting into the room.

Annie sat down on the small bench that matched the vanity. For a little while she'd almost forgotten her ugly secret, then it was in her face again with all the talk about rainbows. She tried to push the thought away by concentrating on what she was going to do when she returned home. If she was lucky, July's profits would allow her to finally make up the money Rosie had chewed to pieces and then she would be able to package it up and return it to the bank. Fourteen months' worth of interest would bankrupt her. She'd have to figure out a way to send an IOU of some kind that couldn't be traced. *Don't think about that now. Think about these beautiful islands and this mini vacation. Think about Parker Grayson. Think about how attracted you are to him. Think about what it would be like to go to bed with him. Right here in this big old four-poster with the gentle trade winds blowing over your slick naked body. Think about* that. A ring of scorching heat circled her neck and crept up to her face just as a knock sounded on her door.

Annie opened the door, her face flaming. She'd never felt so flustered in her life.

"What's wrong?" Parker asked, his voice full of concern.

"Wrong?"

"Yes, you're all flushed."

"Oh. You probably won't believe this but I saw a cobweb up near the molding and I was jumping up and down to swat at it with a towel. Your housekeeper is too old to be jumping up and down."

"You're right, I don't believe you." Parker grinned. "I'd really like to hear the real reason you look so flustered."

The rosy hue on Annie's face darkened. "I don't think you could handle it."

"I'm a big boy. Try me."

"I was wondering what it would be like to go to bed with you," Annie said coolly as she sashayed past him and out through the door. She turned once and called over her shoulder, "Coming?" *Guess you left him speechless, Anna Daisy Clark. He looks absolutely dumbfounded.*

"You were saying," Annie prodded.

"Ah, what I was . . . ah thinking . . ."

"Yes, yes. What were you thinking?" She was enjoying this.

"I'm easy, but I'm not *that* easy."

"Easy is good. Did you ever make love in a bed filled with those wonderful flowers they make the leis with? By the way, all island visitors are supposed to get a lei. I did not get one." She wagged a finger under Parker's nose. Then she smiled wickedly. *This is somebody else in my body. This isn't me saying all these wild things. I never said anything even remotely like what I just said to this man. Never in my whole life.*

"No." The single word exploded from Parker's mouth like a gunshot.

"That's a shame," Annie said. "Which way is the lanai?"

"You're standing in it. Sit!"

"Why?" Annie asked.

"Because I told you to. I'll be right back."

Annie sat. She waited and waited. When her lemonade glass was empty she got up. *Some host. You probably scared him off, Annie Clark.*

"I thought I told you to sit."

"I was sitting. Now I'm standing. What difference does it make? You tell dogs to sit, not people."

"Go ahead, spoil our island traditions. It won't work unless you're sitting. Now sit!"

Annie sat.

"There. Now you have been officially greeted by a native of Hawaii," Parker said, placing not one but two fragrant leis around her neck. "I made them myself. That's what took me so long. Turn around. There's more to the custom." Annie turned around. "Now, close your eyes."

Annie closed her eyes. It was the sweetest, the most demanding, the most wonderful kiss she'd ever received in her life. She never wanted it to end.

Annie licked at her kissed lips. "I liked that."

"And well you should. It was one of my better efforts."

"Effort?"

"You know what I mean. You always save the best till . . . just the right time."

"Which would be . . . when?" *How had an alien being invaded her body? Who was this person saying all these things?*

"Do you want to set a date, or do you think we should get to know one another a little better?"

"I'm a what you see is what you get kind of person, Mr. Grayson. How about you?"

"Does that mean you don't have any deep, dark secrets? Everyone has secrets. People always say they're a what you see is what you get kind of person, then you find out they have all these problems, secrets, baggage, whatever."

Annie could feel her stomach muscles start to tighten up. She tried for a light tone. "Are you saying you're one of those people who is an open book with absolutely no secrets or skeletons in your closet?"

"That's what I'm saying. How about you? By the way, how old are you?"

"How old are *you?*" Annie demanded.

"I asked you first," Parker said.

"Old enough to know better. You're not supposed to ask a woman her age."

"Who said that?"

"My mother said it," Annie shot back. "I'm twenty-five."

"That's a good age," Parker said.

"A good age for what?"

"Starting a business, making love, getting married, having babies. So, are we setting a date or what? We should get it settled before we sit down to business."

"You're making it sound like a business deal," Annie said sourly. "I'm a sharp, intelligent businesswoman, so don't think you can put anything over on me. I can always get my coffee in Sumatra." *Good, the alien being had left her body, and she was now in control again.*

"How does four o'clock tomorrow afternoon sound? My own private beach. We'll go skinny-dipping. Then if it looks like something might come of it, we'll be ready. It will be like *From Here to Eternity.*" He was laughing at her. *The alien being swished through her body again.*

Annie smiled. Ever so sweetly. A wicked gleam in her eye, she said, "I hope you're *up* to it." She dusted her hands dramatically. "That's a really *big* beach down there. I bet it would take a *ton* of these petals to cover it. If there's one thing I hate, it's getting sand up my butt."

Parker choked on the lemonade he was about to swallow. Annie was off her chair in a heartbeat to pound him on his back. "Was it something I said? I love these leis. They make me feel . . . like I should be doing sinful things." *I've lost what's left of my mind. Think about the bank money. That will get you back on track.*

Parker cleared his throat. "I thought I'd give you a rundown on the coffee business before we fly out to Kona tomorrow."

"I'm all ears," Annie said as she propped her elbows on the table. "I hope you're going to tell me something I don't know."

"Daniel didn't say you were a smart-ass."

"Daniel doesn't know me. He's got great buns. Good, sturdy legs, too. He's a nice guy. Not my type, though." *You need to think about Peter Newman and the bank money. He's going to nail you when you get back.*

"Parker, I've been teasing you. I don't know what in the world got into me. I've never behaved this way in my life. I've always been a very boring, bookish person. I take my responsibilities very seriously. Something must have happened to my hormones when I set foot on this island. I apologize for my . . . tacky behavior. I did enjoy the kiss, though. Could we just forget everything that came before and after and concentrate on the reason I'm here."

"How's that going to work? Daniel said you were my destiny. He never lies."

"He does so lie. Everyone lies at some point or another."

"I don't," Parker said virtuously.

"We were going to talk about coffee."

"Fine, let's talk about coffee. For starters, the coffee grown here in Maui is not Kona coffee. The only place in the world that grows Kona coffee is the Kona district of the Big Island. We've been growing it in the rich volcanic soil on the slopes of Mauna Loa and Hualaalai for more than a hundred and fifty years. We tend our trees by hand and we're very selective about the ripe red cherries we pick. After we pick the cherries, the outer skins and pulp are removed in the pulping mill and the beans are put out to dry. When the beans dry completely the outer parchment skin and the inner silverskin are removed. We grade by size and density before we sew them in the burlap bags that carry our certificate. We ship to roasters around the world. We have our own roaster also. It's up to the clients if they want us to roast it or not. If you buy our coffee, do you want us to roast it or will you have it shipped to a roaster on the mainland? That's my spiel. My father made me memorize it when I was a kid. Did it sound rehearsed and flat?"

"Yes, but that's okay. Depends on the price," Annie said. "Kona coffee is expensive. We sell it for twenty-two dollars a pound. I'll sell it to you for sixteen and we roast. Providing you buy in thousand-pound increments. I'll drop an additional two dollars a pound for every additional thousand pounds you buy. How many shops do you have now?"

"Four. Elmo wants to blitz the South. Start-up costs are nil. It's finding the right, trustworthy people. Tom and I can only do so much. Elmo is in his late sixties. So far we have good people. The fact that we open the shops near college campuses helps because kids are always looking for part-time jobs. The downside is it's strictly a cash business. Money is tempting when you're on a short leash."

"What's your control?"

"The cups and the croissants. In the beginning we just served coffee and tuna sandwiches, using Elmo's mother's secret recipe. The control was really tight. Then we included brownies on Mondays and went on to espresso, lattes, and cappuccino. You need more of some coffees and less of others. If I follow Elmo's business plan, and Tom agrees to work his tail off, we could open five more shops by the end of the year. I'll be spending all my time on the road checking on the shops. You should know what I'm talking about. When you own a business, you're married to it. There's no time for anything else. There's no time for a private life. All I've ever done in my life is work. I don't know if I want to go after all this on such a grand scale."

"There's an alternative," Parker said seriously.

"What's that? Move to the islands and drink coconut milk?"

"You could open shops all across the country. Get them started, keep good books, and in a year, sell the franchise. There's big money in that. Go to a good headhunter for managerial positions. That's what I would do if I were in your position.

However, that doesn't mean you have to do it just because I suggested it."

"It makes sense. In the beginning it was kind of a lark. You know, starting your own business with very little money and then, bam, it just took off. I wasn't prepared for it, and neither was Jane. In the end it was too much for her. My brother came back at just the right moment. It's certainly something to think about. I'm going to have to call my brother to talk to him about the prices you offered."

"Take all the time you need. My coffee beans and I aren't going anywhere. There was a time when more than ten million pounds of Kona coffee was produced each year. Today there are less than two million pounds being produced. It's the rarest of the rare. We want to keep it that way. That concludes our business for the day. Let's have some fun."

Annie grew still. "What do you mean by fun?"

"Explore the island. Run under the falls. Jump in the water. Climb the monkeypod tree, come back, take a nap. Separately, of course. Get dressed up, go out to dinner and then come home and go to bed. Separately, of course. Rise and shine in the morning, eat a wonderful breakfast, after which I will fly us to Kona and give you a tour of my coffee plantation. How does that sound?"

"Should I change? Do you treat all your prospective customers like this?"

"Sneakers and shorts would be good. No. Most of them are stuffy old ducks who want everything for nothing. You're my first beautiful female customer. Plus, Daniel said you were my destiny, so I have to find out if he's right."

"Okay. Give me ten minutes. Daniel needs to mind his own business."

"Five."

"You got it." Annie giggled.

*   *   *

"It s been a wonderful afternoon, Parker. I had fun, I feel rested, and I learned a lot. You're a very good tour guide. I never hid behind a waterfall before. I feel invisible."

"I used to hide here from my father when I was little. At least I thought I was hiding until he told me he used to do the same thing. This big old stone we're resting in is like a chair. That leads me to believe hundreds of children over the years did the same thing we're doing. How is it you never had time for fun, Annie? Look! Now, I'd say that's something special! Just for you, Annie. We should call it Annie's Rainbow. I've been coming here since I was three years old, and I never saw a prettier one. It's bigger, more vibrant and can be seen for miles. I guess it's your special welcome to Maui."

Annie stared at the rainbow, a chill running up and down her arms. She squinted to see through the shimmering waterfall. Where did it end and what was in the pot of gold here in this beautiful paradise? She shivered again. Parker put his arm around her shoulders. "I never had a rainbow named after me. To answer your question about fun, first my dad got sick, then my mom got . . . she has Alzheimer's disease. We didn't know what it was at first. Tom was in college, so I had to take care of Mom while I was in high school. I had to rush home after school. Baby-sitters for older people are expensive. Mom got worse, and we had to put her in a nursing home, and that was expensive. We sold the house to pay off Dad's sky-high medical bills and our share for Mom's care. Their savings went to pay for Tom's college tuition. There wasn't any left for me, so I had to work my way through. Thank God for Elmo. If you ever want to know anything about the drugstore business, just ask me. I had a mountain of student loans. It all turned around when we opened the first shop. If there were more hours in the day, I could have tripled my money. I went to bed tired and woke up tired. This is the first vacation I've had in seven years. Not only that, it's tax deductible. At least the airfare is. If your next question is, did I ever have boyfriends or relationships, the answer is yes but time ruined all of them.

"Having my own business where I didn't have to answer to anyone was always a dream of mine. I did the college thing because both Mom and Dad wanted Tom and me to have degrees since they didn't have the opportunity to go to college. The business helped move Mom closer to me, and the facility is really great. I get to see her weekends. I told myself I was giving it three years, and if I didn't make it by then, I would look for a nine-to-five job. Sitting behind a desk is not what I'm all about. Jane felt the same way. All she wants to do is paint. She's looking forward to having kids. She was a foster-home child, so having her own family is very important to her. Do you have any idea how lucky you are, Parker?"

"Yes. Sometimes it seems a little hollow. Life should be shared."

"How is it you aren't married?"

Parker laughed. "I came close several times. It didn't feel right, so each time I broke it off."

"Do you run everything? Why do your sisters live on the mainland? Don't you miss them?"

"Of course I miss them. I inherited because I'm the oldest male child. It's tradition."

Annie's eyes snapped open and she sat up. "Wait right there. Are you saying all of this belongs to you and not your sisters? Do you share the profits with them?"

"Our traditions here are different from what you're used to. It's our way."

"That's incredible, and it certainly isn't fair. You get everything, and they get nothing?" Something in Annie snapped. There was such outrage in her voice, Parker reared back. "Aren't they bitter?"

"Bitter? I don't think so. They're all very well off. They moved by choice."

"Well, hell, I'd move, too," Annie exploded. "That's exactly what happened to me through no fault of my parents. Tom got it all. I had to bust my ass. I don't want to hear any crap about it building character, either. You can't take character to the bank. I used to eat mayonnaise sandwiches and drink Kool-Aid. That sure as hell didn't build my character. I was always hungry."

"Wait just a damn minute. You're making it sound like I cheated my sisters. I didn't. It was all laid out. I told you, it's our tradition."

"Your tradition stinks. What that says to me is women don't count. If they counted, you would have shared. You live like a king in this beautiful paradise. They grew up here, too. Another thing, *Mr. Coffee*, remember that it was a *woman* who gave birth to you. I've just decided I don't think I like you. And I sure as hell don't like all these traditions you're steeped in. I made the mistake of letting this stray off the business path. I can't respect you now. I'm sorry."

Parker Grayson stared at his destiny with disbelieving eyes. "Just hold on here, Miss Clark. What you don't seem to understand is no one is complaining. Furthermore, it's none of your business."

"You're right, it is none of my business. Why would your sisters complain? What good would it do? They have to accept it since they have no other choice. What do you do for them?"

"Do?"

"When you inherited all of this, what did you do for them?"

"I didn't do anything. They didn't want me to do anything. They got married and had babies. That was what they wanted to do."

"Scrooge! Don't deny it. That's exactly what you are. Would it hurt you to share your good fortune with them? You know what, I hated my brother for a long time. Deep-down, gut hatred. It started to consume me. I had to let it go for my own survival."

"My sisters aren't like you. I don't mean that the way it sounds," Parker said, a helpless look on his face.

"How do you know? Did you ever ask? How many sisters do you have?"

"No, I never asked. I have six sisters. They all have well-to-do husbands."

"One seventh of something is a lot less than the whole of something. And, they probably don't have a dime in their own names."

"Where is this coming from? We were having such a good time. Why do my sisters need to have money in their own names?"

"For the same reason I do. Parents have no right to do that to their children. You are no better than your parents. One of your sisters, given the chance, might have been a whiz at running your coffee company. Maybe you're right, and maybe they don't care. I care, and that's all that's important. Women are not second-class citizens. I can't believe you went to school on the mainland. This is the eighties, Mr. Grayson. Women no longer take a backseat to men. I want to go home, and I want to go home *now!*"

"Fine," Parker snapped. "Watch your footing, or you'll go into the falls."

"God, I just hate it when people disappoint me," Annie seethed.

"What?"

"Shut up. I wasn't talking to you," Annie continued to fume.

The trip to the plantation house was made in silence. When Parker held the door open for her, Annie marched inside and down the long hall to her room. "Damn!" Her bags had been unpacked. Now she had to pack them again. She did it any old way. The sound of the zipper closing was so loud in the room, Annie found herself wincing. "Just when I thought I found the perfect man he turns out to be a dud. Damn, damn, damn!"

"This is stupid, Annie," Parker said.

"Yes, I could see how it would seem stupid to you," Annie said. "Who's taking me to the airport?"

"It looks like I'm the lucky winner."

The housekeeper looked from one angry face to the other. Hesitantly, she held out a rainbow-colored gown. Tears welled in Annie's eyes as she reached for it. "Thank you so much for . . . for this." She slung the dress over her shoulder as she made her way to the front door.

"She doesn't understand our ways. She's upset because I inherited the plantation and my sisters didn't," Parker whispered to the old woman.

"Miss Clark is right, Parker. It was a terrible thing your parents did to your sisters. The old ways no longer work, as my children point out to George and me on a daily basis. It is a new time we live in, Parker. If we are to grow with the times, then we must embrace that same time. Why do you close your eyes to this? You were educated on the mainland at great expense. I can speak like this, Parker, because I raised you along with your mother, and when she was no longer here, I raised you alone. Now, go to the young lady and make peace. She looked very angry to me. She is the best one yet. As George says, you snooze, you lose. Go now, Parker."

"We'll discuss this later in *greater* detail, Mattie," Parker hissed in the old housekeeper's ear.

Mattie drew herself tall until she was eyeball-to-eyeball with Parker. "No. I have said all I intend to say. If you wish to discuss the matter, it should be with your sisters."

"I'll be damned. When did you go modern on me, Mattie?"

"When I learned about social security, pension plans, and

estate planning. Sometimes I think you have coffee beans for brains. I told you to go, Parker!''

''Yes, ma'am,'' Parker said, turning on his heel. It didn't pay to argue with either Mattie or George.

In the car, Parker reached up to the visor for his aviator glasses. Behind the dark shades he felt more confident. Out of the corner of his eye he could see how straight Annie was sitting, how prim and proper she looked. He slammed the car into gear. "Listen, you can't just barge into my life, tell me what to do, then barge back out because you don't like my culture. I wouldn't even think about doing something like that to you. What the hell kind of destiny is this?''

''I don't have any trouble with your culture. It's your attitude about women. Let's just say for the sake of argument that you and I got married. I have a successful business. You have a successful business. We have one boy and two girls. Who gets our estate when we die?''

''I got the point back at the falls.''

''Who gets the estate, Parker?''

''The oldest son.''

''My business, too?''

''Yours becomes mine at marriage.''

''Stop this fucking car right now. I'll walk the rest of the way, thank you.''

Parker's foot slammed on the brake. ''You can send me my bags.'' Hands on hips, Annie glared at the man behind the sunglasses. ''Do not ever, even for one second, think I would bust my ass working sixteen or eighteen hours a day so *your* son could inherit over *my* daughters.''

''We aren't married,'' Parker bellowed.

''Damn right we aren't, and we aren't going to get married, either. I wouldn't marry you with your archaic ideas if you were the last man on earth!''

"Get in this damn car before I pick you up and throw you in it," Parker bellowed again.

"Kiss my ass, Parker Grayson."

"Where did you learn to talk like that? You should be ashamed of yourself."

"From my brother and his friends. I am not ashamed of myself. Now, get the hell out of my way before I push that car you're sitting in over the edge."

From the set of her jaw and the murderous look in her eye, Parker knew she meant business. A sick feeling settled in the pit of his stomach. In the few hours they'd spent together, he'd realized he really liked the feisty young woman. There was no doubt in his mind that Daniel was right. He could see the two of them watching their children growing up, traveling together, growing old together. *Is she right? If she is, what does that make me? Mattie would say a horse's patoot.*

"Fine, do it your way, Miss Smart-Ass."

"I'd rather be a smart-ass than a jackass," Annie shot back. *Shit, shit, shit. How could something so perfect suddenly turn so ugly and hateful?* Was she overreacting? Of course she was, but she wasn't backing down. She'd had it with people, men in particular, who thought of women as second-class citizens.

What seemed like an eternity later, Annie limped into the airport parking lot, Parker gliding along behind her in the plantation car. "Just put my bags on the curb."

Parker stood facing her. He removed his sunglasses. "If my father were alive, he'd take a switch to me for allowing you to walk to the airport."

"Is that the same father who cut his daughters out of his will? If so, forget it. I've walked longer distances in my life."

"Annie, I'm sorry. I'm not sure what it is I'm sorry about. If it's a word, I've said it. You don't understand."

A second later Annie was in his face. "You see, you're wrong. I do understand. What I understand is you are a greedy son of a bitch like my brother Tom was. I forgave him because he's my brother. You, on the other hand, have no excuses. You probably have more money than I could ever dream about. I'll just bet you a thousand pounds of coffee if we planned on getting married the first two words out of your mouth would be prenuptial agreement. Ah, I see by the stricken look on your face I'm right. Now, that's a modern, eighties legal agreement. Why would that be good enough for you and yet the old way of disinheriting your sisters is still good. I rest my case. If I decide to buy your coffee, I'll be in touch.''

"Annie, we're both adults. Can't we go into the bar, sit down, and talk? I'd like to try and explain the way it is.''

She was in his face again, their noses almost touching. "I'll tell you what, Parker Grayson. You go talk to your sisters. Be an honest, open, big brother and ask them what they think and feel and how they felt when they knew they were cut off because they were *just women*. If they tell you it's fine with them, call me and I'll come back here. I'd like to meet six women who feel like you *think* they do. If I prove right, you supply my coffee for a full year. *Free*. Here,'' she said, throwing the leis he'd made for her, at him.

Annie stalked off. Parker watched her until she was out of sight. Suddenly the sun dimmed and the sick feeling returned to the pit of his stomach. He wished he was a little boy again so he could cry.

CHAPTER SEVEN

"You don't seem very happy, Parker. Is something wrong?"
Mattie asked. "The house is in readiness. I cooked everything
you asked me to cook. The presents for your sisters are all
under the tree. It is a joyful time. You always loved Christmas,
so why don't we sit down and talk about it? I would have to
be blind as well as deaf not to know you haven't been the same
since Miss Clark left, back in July. Five months is a very long
time, Parker. I've never asked what went wrong. Sometimes
talking about things helps."

"There isn't all that much to talk about, Mattie. Nothing
much has changed. Miss Clark's visit was for business purposes.
She chastised me for the way I do . . . did things. The truth is,
my culture is none of her business. She's one of those modern
eighties women everyone talks about. I did like her tremen-
dously until she started . . . It's not important. I don't think I
could ever feel the same about her. She was so . . . I don't
know, brash, uncouth, so . . . mainland.''

"Do not tell me a lie, Parker. Your eyes tell me something different. You never did talk to your sisters, did you?"

"No. I was going to do that today. They didn't want to come, Mattie. I guess that bothers me."

"This is the first time you invited your sisters to their old home in many years. Why would you think they should be overjoyed to visit you now?"

"They have husbands and children. I thought, old times, memories, that sort of thing might appeal to them. They wouldn't come for dinner, so I settled for lunch. They want to leave right afterward, which tells me I should have scuttled the whole idea the moment it entered my mind."

"And that surprises you?"

"Doesn't it surprise you, Mattie?"

"No. One always wants to know they can go home. This was your sisters' home as well as yours. When you returned from the mainland it became *your* home. There is a piece of paper in the courthouse that says this is so. Your sisters have never come here uninvited. Your nieces and nephews know nothing of this beautiful place. Once you went surfing with them, Parker. Once."

"There aren't enough hours in the day for me to keep going back and forth to the Big Island. They have fathers. They have each other."

"And you wonder why they don't wish to join you for this little luncheon. I think you just answered your own question."

"I guess what you're trying to tell me is my sisters don't like me very much."

"That is an accurate assessment, Parker."

"Do they resent me, Mattie?"

"Yes, Parker, they do."

"Then why didn't they say something? Why didn't *you* say something?"

"It wasn't my place."

"The hell it wasn't. You don't have the least bit of trouble telling me anything else. Why couldn't you tell me that?"

"That is family business. It is not *my* business. When was the last time you called any of your sisters just to say hello, how are you? I see. The answer is never."

"I have to leave now to pick them up at the airport."

"Where are the leis?"

"Leis?" Parker said, a stupid look on his face.

Exasperated, Mattie said, "Yes, leis for your sisters. It would be the nice thing to do. It is, after all, our custom."

"They live here, Mattie. They aren't coming from the mainland."

Mattie's shoulders stiffened. "You will wait right here, Parker, and you will not move," she said sternly. She was back almost instantly with six breathtaking leis. "I made them a short while ago. You will place one around each sister's neck and kiss her cheek. Do you understand me, Parker?"

"Yes, ma'am."

"Be sure to tell them how pretty they are. They are, you know."

"I know that," Parker said, shuffling his feet. "Is there anything else, Mattie, that's lacking in the manners department?"

"Ask George."

They weren't just pretty, they were beautiful. And they were his sisters. For a moment, Parker felt overwhelmed when they walked toward him. They waited expectantly as he draped a lei around each of them and then kissed them. "I'm glad you came," he said sincerely. He waited for them to respond and when they didn't, he ushered them through the airport and out to his waiting car.

They sat stiffly and primly, much the way Annie had sat

back in the summer, when he'd driven her to the airport. This was not going to be an easy visit. The six of them responded when he spoke to them but volunteered nothing to the conversation. He was relieved when they reached the house. He stepped back when all six of them ran to Mattie and George, who welcomed them with open arms. There was nothing shy about them now. They chattered and giggled like little girls, the little sisters he remembered. He suddenly felt like an outsider when he heard Lela, the oldest say, "My God, this banyan tree is bigger than the house. I remember the day Mama planted it. She said it would grow big and strong like . . . Parker."

"Guess she was right about that," Teke, the second oldest said. "What's with this command performance, Mattie? I wanted to tell him to stuff his invitation, but Lela said we had to come." A deep frown etched itself on Parker's forehead at his sister's biting words.

"I don't want any fruit punch, Mattie. However, I'll take a double shot of Jack Daniel's on the rocks," Cassie said.

"I'll have a beer," Mahala said boisterously.

"Me too," Jana said.

"Scotch on the rocks for me," Kiki, the youngest said. "Smells good in here. Whatcha making, Mattie?"

"All your favorites," Mattie replied.

"Why?" the six sisters asked in unison.

"Your brother asked me to," Mattie said flatly.

Kiki whirled around. "Okay, big brother, now that you have us here, what's the drill? What do you want from us? You already have everything. In case you need a transfusion, count me out." Parker listened in horror as the rest of his sisters muttered the same words.

"Why don't we go into the library and have a little talk before lunch. Bring your drinks."

"Nice tree," Lela said, walking past the Christmas tree. "It's bigger than my whole living room."

"You must have a lot of friends or are all those presents for Mattie and George?" Teke said.

This was not going the way he'd planned. "Actually, they're for all of you."

"Really," Kiki drawled. "We didn't bring one for you. That means we can't accept yours. Money is always tight around this time of year. 'Course you wouldn't know anything about that, would you, Parker?"

Money was tight around this time of year. That didn't make any sense. "I didn't expect you to bring me a present."

"Let's cut the bullshit, Parker, and get to the chase. Why are we here?" Kiki said, gulping at her drink.

"What happened to you? What happened to all of you? You were never like this. You're Hawaiian women. You talk like . . ." For one split second he was going to say, like Annie. "It's not nice," he said lamely.

"We grew up. Guess you didn't notice. You being so busy here running things and all," Jana said tightly.

Parker stared at his sisters. He thought he saw disgust on all their faces. Disgust with him. It was all a bad dream. Annie Clark was preying on his mind and taking her revenge on him through his dreams. He shook his head to try to clear his thoughts. "Let's all sit down. I want to talk to you about something that concerns all of us."

"You know what, Parker, you're about ten years too late. None of us gives a shit what you want or don't want. Ah, I see my language offends you. That's just tough. Spit it out. What do you want from us? Wait a minute, I know what he wants," Lela said as she whirled around to face her sisters. "He wants absolution. Guess what, big brother, we're fresh out. That about sums up our contribution to this little visit. You called, we came, and now we're going. We can get a burger in town. George can drive us back to the airport."

Parker's jaw dropped when all six sisters set their glasses down on cue and turned to follow Lela to the door.

"Goddamn it! Get back here and sit down. I told you I want to talk to you. You're going to sit and listen whether you like it or not."

Teke whirled around at the speed of light. With her index finger she jabbed at the center of her brother's neck. "You see, that's where you're wrong. You gave up the right to tell any of us what to do. What do you say, girls, should we let him have it?"

They converged on him as one, backing him up to the sofa and pushing him down. Teke walked around to the back and held his shoulders to prevent him from getting up. Her grip was like a vise.

It wasn't a dream, it was a black, ugly nightmare. And from the looks of things he wasn't going to wake up anytime soon.

"I think I'll go first since I'm the oldest," Lela said.

The others nodded as they picked up their drinks. They were smiling now at his discomfort. The funny thing was, in his dream each one of his sisters looked like Annie Clark. Only it wasn't a dream.

"When you were born, Parker, this house was full of joy and happiness. It was like Christmas. Mama's miracle son. We were just little girls then, but we remember. Five days after your birth, Mama planted the banyan tree. I was holding you in my arms as we watched her dig out the dirt. It was something she had to do. Of course we didn't understand what it all meant to her. By planting the tree she thought you would live forever. She had become very frail and was too old to have a child at that time. Like most women, she wanted to give her husband a son.

"*We* raised you, Parker, not Mama, not Mattie. We did it because we loved you. We pulled you around in the wagon, we taught you to swim, to jump in the pools, hide behind the falls. We taught you to climb the monkeypod tree and taught you how to ride your first bicycle and when you fell off you had six nurses in attendance. We made sure you brushed your teeth and took your bath. We even followed you on your first dates and hid in the bushes so you wouldn't see us. We begged and pleaded with Papa until he couldn't stand our pestering, to get you your first car. We combed your hair and took you to church. We showered you with love and shared everything in our lives with you.

"And then, one day, you didn't need us anymore. Papa decided it was time for *you* to learn the coffee business because one day it would be all *yours*. Mama died, and Papa decided it was time to marry us all off. We didn't have anything to say about it. I wanted to be a schoolteacher. Teke wanted to study music. Jana wanted to be an artist. Cassie had dreams of being an entertainer. Mahala wanted to study law. Kiki was the one who wanted to learn the coffee business. None of our dreams came true.

"We mistakenly thought when Papa died that you would share your life and your fortune with us. Did I leave anything out?"

"Only that we hate his guts," Kiki said, finishing her drink.

Parker flinched. "I thought you were all married and happy. You never came here. I thought . . ."

"It's the same old bullshit," Teke said.

"Why are we bothering with this? Let's go back to town," Cassie said.

Teke yanked at her brother's head pulling it backward. She leaned down, her eyes boring into his. "You're never going to be happy, Parker. In your heart, tradition and culture be damned. You know you were wrong. We were part of this family long before you came along. You think about that while we go back to town."

"Okay, enough is enough!" Parker roared. "I don't need

to think about it. That's all I've done for the past five months.
All of you are right. Yes, I was deaf, dumb, blind, and stupid.
When you didn't say anything, I accepted the fact that you
accepted the conditions of Papa's will. I never knew you had
hopes and dreams. That in itself was incredibly stupid on my
part. I thought all you wanted was to get married and have
families. Again, that was stupid on my part. I want to make it
right. I will make it right. It's not too late. I want us to share
equally and evenly. I want you to know you can come here to
this house anytime you want. You do not need an invitation.
Your rooms are just like they were when you left. Mattie kept
them that way for you. I'd like all your children to come here
and enjoy the same life you had when you lived here. I'm just
sorry it's taken me so long to do this. The business will now
have seven equal partners. Kiki, if you want, I could really use
an assistant. If you don't like that word, how would you like
to be working partner.''

"What's the catch? Why are you being so generous all of
a sudden?" Jana asked.

"What do we have to do in return for this generosity?"
Mahala asked suspiciously.

"Just be my sisters and give me the chance to be your
brother. There's room on this estate to build a dozen houses.
Pick your spot. I'll have the houses built to your specifications.''

"Of course this will all be done legally," Mahala said.

"Of course. It's not too late for any of you to follow your
dreams.''

"Yes, Parker, it's too late. We're willing to forgo our dreams
so that our children can follow theirs. My son wants to be a
lawyer. It takes a great deal of money to go to law school on
the mainland," Mahala said.

"I should have known that," Parker muttered.

"Yes, you should have," Lela said.

"Will you stay?" Parker asked.

"Yes, Parker, we'll stay," Kiki said. "I'm going to take you up on your offer to work at the plantation. I have some great ideas."

"I'd like to hear them. First, though, I have something I have to do. If you like, you can watch. Meet me outside by the front door."

The sisters looked at one another and shrugged as they trekked through the house to the front foyer and then out the door. They squealed in horror when they saw Parker swing the ax at the base of the old banyan tree. "Why are you doing this?" they shouted.

"Because it's a symbol of everything that went wrong with us. No one lives forever. If there were seven right in a row, I'd leave them be. One is no good. George can grind out the stump, and we'll decide what kind of welcoming plant we want by our front door."

When the giant tree toppled to the ground there were shouts of approval. George and Mattie clapped their hands. "One more thing," Parker said. "Last one up the monkeypod tree is a horse's patoot!"

High-heeled shoes sailed through the air as the Grayson siblings ran around the house to the side yard. "You remembered!" they shouted in glee.

They were slick and they were fast as they shinnied up the old knurled tree. Parker was the last to straddle the long, twisted branch.

"Merry Christmas!" Parker gasped.

"Merry Christmas!" his sisters shouted.

Annie tore the cellophane from the new calendar. She crossed her fingers that 1982 would be as good a year as the previous one. She sipped at the wine in her glass, her right hand tickling Rosie behind her ears. The shepherd stared at her with adoring eyes. "It's just you and me, girl. I thought he would at least send a Christmas card. I think the hardest thing was going to lunch with Daniel before Christmas and not asking about Parker. I wanted him to say something so bad, and he didn't. So much for destiny and love and all that garbage. When you're right, you're right. When you're wrong, you're wrong. I'm not some dumb female that needs a man in her life. It would be nice, but it's not necessary. I really liked him, Rosie. He's a great kisser, too. The best so far," she clarified. "He even named a rainbow after me. Then, bam, it was all over. Come on, get your leash and let's go for a long walk along the battery. I'm going to buy a house there someday. I'm going to get us one of those big old houses with a walled-in courtyard where you can romp and play to your heart's content. I'm going to get you a playmate, too.''

The shepherd pranced over to the coatrack and daintily removed her leash.

"You're so beautiful you belong on a calendar. Maybe I'll look into that. After I open the next six stores. That's going to make sixteen stores in total. When we come back after our walk, you and I are going to talk about *that money* because Mr. Peter Newman is still sniffing around. I've reconciled myself to the fact the man is never going to go away." Annie snapped the leash onto Rosie's harness and left by the back door.

When they turned the corner leading to their street at three o'clock, Rosie strained at her leash. She growled and bared her teeth when she saw the man sitting on the stoop waiting for them. "Easy girl. We can deal with him."

"I thought I told you to call before you came here. I'm much too busy to talk to you today, and I have nothing new to say to you. What that means is, get off my property or I'm calling the police. I'll get a restraining order if I have to."

"I have something new to report to you. We finished up our investigation before Christmas. We have successfully eliminated every car owner but you, Miss Abbott, and Elmo Richardson. We're satisfied that there was no third party. We became satisfied when we offered a deal to the young man in jail. He couldn't take advantage of it to cut down on his prison time, because there was no third party. That brought us back to the cars on the street and the campus parking lot. It is my personal belief that the money was tossed into Jane Abbott's car, you covered up for her, and Elmo Richardson took care of the money. Sooner or later, I'll be able to prove it."

Annie fought the urge to put her fist through Peter Newman's face.

Rosie sensed her owner's fear and lunged at the investigator. It was all Annie could do to hold the huge dog in check. "Get off my property. If you think I'm guilty of something besides leaving my car windows open, charge me or get the hell off my property and don't come back. I don't have anything else to say to you, not now, not ever. Are we clear on that matter?"

Her insides shaking like Jell-O, Annie led Rosie up the steps and into the house. She unhooked the leash, locked and double-bolted the front door. She ran to the back door and did the same thing before she took the steps two at a time to the second floor, where she fell onto the bed gasping for breath. She needed to calm down and call Jane. And Elmo. And Tom. And the police. Another call to the insurance company and one to her lawyer would not be out of order either. When you were guilty you had to act like you were innocent. No, she couldn't call Tom. Tom would suspect immediately. He'd been as good as his word when she came up with the hundred thousand dollars to pay off his ex-wife for the kids.

The scheme had been elaborate, and it had worked. Mona, so greedy for the money, would have done anything to get it. Tom had told her he borrowed it. There was nothing in writing; the payment had been in cash. Mona had promised never to interfere in the children's lives. A month after she sold the house, keeping all the equity, Mona had disappeared off the face of the earth. The children now lived with Tom and a part-time housekeeper in North Carolina. Everyone was healthy and happy.

Except for the Boston National Bank, who still hadn't gotten their money back. As soon as the accounting firm gave her a date to take the last quarter's profits, Annie would pay back the bank. Everything was ready to go. The moment she had the remaining money from the hundred thousand dollars, which amounted to thirty-three thousand, she would ship the money back. This time there would be no more delays. Tom was already paying her back and didn't take a year-end bonus even though there was more than enough in their business account.

Annie sighed. Life was never dull.

Rosie watched her mistress until she was certain her breathing was under control. Only then did she lie down, her head between her paws, her eyes bright and alert.

Suddenly, Annie wanted to cry, as her thoughts carried her to a faraway place behind a silvery, shimmering waterfall. She wondered then, as she had a thousand times before, if she'd overreacted. She'd picked up the phone to call Parker at least a hundred times only to replace it at the last second. There was something wrong there. She just didn't know exactly what it was. Then, of course, there was her pride. Pride was a terrible thing.

Time to call Jane and ruin her day. "Hey, Jane," she said a moment later, "how's my best friend? Wonderful. Happy New Year, Jane! I love this time of year, when the shops are closed for the school breaks. Oh, I'm not doing much. I hang out with Rosie. We just came in from our walk, and guess who was sitting on my front steps. I have bad news, Jane. Mr. Newman has decided through the process of elimination that the money went into your car, I covered up for you, and Elmo kept the money bag. He didn't say so, but I think he thinks we split it among ourselves. He said something new this time around. He said they offered to cut a deal with the kid in prison to lighten his sentence if he would tell who the third person was. The kid said there was no third person. That brought them back to the cars that had open windows. If there was a third person, the boy would have gone for the deal. This is what we're looking at, Jane. I'm calling the police to get a restraining order on him, and I think you should do the same thing. I'm also going to call the insurance company again or have my lawyer do it. I just wanted you to be prepared. They have no proof, Jane. Any lawyer would have us out on bail in five minutes. No prosecutor would take this case. It's now a cat-and-mouse, wait-and-see game he's playing with us. My books are in order. Every shop we opened was opened the same way as the first one. I pay my taxes, salaries, and the rest is mine. You can't argue with the numbers and numbers are proof. I suppose he thinks we stashed the money somewhere and will spend it sooner or later. He isn't going to give up. I want you to know that. Statute of limitations? I don't know anything about stuff like that. I'll ask the lawyer when I speak to him.

"Mom's fine. Tom is fine, too. The kids are getting big. Mona found herself some young hunk who wants to party like she does. Tom hasn't heard from her. Tom's a great father. I don't want to talk about Parker Grayson, Jane. There's nothing to tell. I hoped he would send a Christmas card, but he didn't. I didn't send one, either. I had lunch with Daniel Christmas week and he didn't bring up Parker's name. I didn't either. We buy our coffee from him, though. Tom handles that end of it. He says I'm too emotional when it comes to Parker. I almost thought he was the one, Jane. I really did. Something didn't, I don't know, jell, I guess for want of a better word. Then I blew it out of the water, and now I'm going to be an old maid. I hear the baby. I have to hang up anyway. Take care, say hello to Bob for me. Bye, Jane.''

* * *

On March 1, the day after four bombs rocked Wall Street in New York City, Annie walked downstairs to the basement, where she'd secured the Boston National Bank's money, dressed in her plastic raincoat that zipped up the front, her hair wrapped in Saran wrap and her hands in latex gloves. No hairs or fibers were going to get anywhere near the money she was about to package up and return to the bank. All the money had gone through the washing machine not once, not twice, but three times. She now sported a brand new General Electric washer and dryer and had switched her brand of soap just in case there was some residue left over in the machine from the money.

The box was huge, but then so was the pile of money in the three dark green trash bags. She'd worked diligently with her calculator trying to figure out, to the penny, the interest the bank lost while the money was in her possession. The biggest problem facing her now was how and where to mail the box of money once she packaged it up. If she was smart, which she wasn't, she would drive to Boston and leave the box on the bank's doorstep. She could leave now and drive through the night, turn around, and drive back. If she swilled coffee all day and night she could probably pull it off. Or she could drive to a distant city and take the box to the nearest post office or UPS with money taped to the box for shipping costs.

Postal authorities would probably think it was a bomb. That would call in the FBI. Damn, why was it so hard to return money? Maybe what she needed to do was make smaller boxes, boxes similar to shirt boxes that would fit into a mailbox on any street corner. If she had the right postage on each package, it would work.

Annie headed for the attic and the empty boxes she'd saved from Christmas. She panicked then. Everyone's fingerprints were on the boxes. Tom's, hers, the kids', Elmo's, her mother's. Rosie's pawprints were sure to be on some of them as she'd trampled through the papers and empty boxes. She was back to square one.

At ten-thirty, Annie loaded three green double-bagged lawn bags containing half of the bank's money into the trunk of her car. She wanted to return all of it, but something perverse inside her warned her to keep the other half. For the time being. Her destination—Atlanta, Georgia. On a plain white envelope tied to the string on each bag was the message: PLEASE RETURN TO BOSTON NATIONAL BANK AS SOON AS POSSIBLE. In smaller letters, she pasted the address of the bank.

It was a five-and-a-half-hour drive to Atlanta. She'd wait around, leave the money at the first bank she came to, then drive back home. She'd be back by noon the following day. Back in September, when she'd planned on returning the money, she'd thought ahead and purchased two cans of gasoline. That would see her to Atlanta and back. No one would even know she was gone. If anyone did come by or call and found her gone, she could say she had taken to her bed with an excruciating headache.

"Okay, Rosie, you have to stay here. I'll put down some papers for you. There's enough food and water to last you till I get back. I'd take you, but someone might remember seeing us together. You stay here and keep your eye on things." The big dog stared at her with unblinking eyes. At one point, Annie thought the dog nodded.

A baseball cap jammed on her head, and wearing an old windbreaker, Annie loaded up the car. At the last moment she stuck her wallet with her license and registration in the hip pocket of her jeans.

Ten minutes later she was headed south on the interstate.

Five hours later Annie cruised past the Georgia National Bank. She drove up and down the street twice to get a feel for

car traffic as well as any pedestrian traffic on their way to an
early-morning job. On her third cruise-by, with no traffic behind
her, she pulled into the parking lot and around to the back of
the bank. She turned off her lights, waited five minutes to see
if anyone had noticed her. Satisfied that she wasn't the object
of anyone's attention, she moved like lightning, wedging the
bags as close to the door as possible. Janitors always reported
early for work. She crossed her fingers that the janitor assigned
to this bank was an honest man.

At 6:35 she was back on the interstate, headed north.

Annie walked in the door of her house at 11:10 to be greeted
boisterously by Rosie. She tussled with her for a few moments
before she hooked the leash onto her harness and led her outside.
"A quick one, girl. I can't believe you held it in this long.
That's what the paper was for. God, I wish you could talk. Did
anyone call or stop by? Good girl. Okay, time to go in."

The phone rang just as Annie pulled some eggs and bacon
from the refrigerator. It was Jane. Annie made her voice as
cheerful as she could. "Hi, how's it going? Did I hear what?
I didn't have the television on this morning. Why? Wow! No
kidding! Are you sure? Wait, I'll turn it on. What station? Wait
a minute, you're three hours behind me. I'll catch the next
newscast. I can't believe it! Somebody just left three bags of
money at a bank in Georgia. Only half but with interest, too?
That's amazing. Oh, well, it's not our problem. So, how's the
weather out there? You lucky dog. It's thirty-six degrees here.
I'm going to light the fireplace. I'm working one to nine today.
Do you ever miss the shop, Jane? No, no word from Parker
Grayson. I haven't seen Daniel either. I can't worry about that
now. Those six new shops we're opening are taking up all my
time. Oh, Jane, listen to this. Tom had a brilliant idea, and he
had these little cards made up asking customers what they liked
about the shop and what drew them to it. Guess what they said!
The daisy awnings over the doors and the daisies we painted

on the walls. The coffee, of course. Since it was your idea, I thought you'd like to know. Okay, I'll let you go. I have to get ready for work. I'll turn on the news tonight when I get home. It's good news, Jane. I know you were worried. Rest easy now. Talk to you soon.''

Annie literally tripped up the steps to the shower where she sang at the top of her lungs. Rosie howled her distress at her off-key singing. "Can't help it, Rosie. I feel like the weight of the world has been taken off my shoulders. We are almost home free, my friend. Now we can concentrate on living our lives instead of a lie. The best part of this whole deal is I never spent one penny of that money on myself. Yes, yes, I used two hundred dollars of it that first week, but I paid it back in a few days. It wasn't for me personally. I didn't let greed take over. I suppose they could hang me for the money I gave Tom to give Mona or the money I used to get Mom situated. So, I used a little of it for a few of the shops. I put it back within a month. I'll have to live with that one. The end justifies the means in that case. The kids are happy with Tom. Tom's happy. Our bills are paid, and I can sing again.

"Life is lookin' good, Rosie. Real good!''

Dressed in a woolly robe, her feet tucked under her, Rosie at her side, Annie stared into the flames as she waited for the eleven o'clock news. She was breathing hard and felt jittery. She knew Tom and Elmo were also glued to the television screen.

The segment was so short, Annie felt cheated. A few seconds of the bank president saying how delighted he was that half the money had come back. Then a short clip of Peter Newman taking credit for putting the fear of God into people his insurance company felt were suspects. His bulldog countenance intensified when the reporter asked him to comment on the fact that interest was paid on the money. He offered a curt "no comment."

Just as Annie was about to turn off the television, a clip came on of an interview with the young man sitting in jail for the crime. He looked more fierce than Peter Newman. She found herself starting to shake when she heard the man say he had his own suspicions and would follow them up when he was released. He also said he had cooperated fully and completely with Peter Newman the insurance investigator. "This is not over," he said belligerently. Annie turned off the set and threw the remote control clear across the room. She was still shaking when Rosie wiggled and squirmed until she was half on her lap and half off. Annie hugged her tightly. She should have returned all the money. Why in the name of God was she keeping it?

"It is so over. I gave half of it back. It's done."

Rosie growled deep in her throat.

"Yeah, girl, that's how I feel."

CHAPTER EIGHT

Eleven years later

Annie hated hospitals. She hated the crisp white uniforms worn by everyone, hated the antiseptic smell that made her want to gag. Worst of all was the knowledge that people died in hospitals. She thought about the endless hours she'd spent in the hospital when her father was so sick and the five-minute rush down the hall just three short months ago when her mother was rushed to the emergency room only to die a few minutes later. Now it was Tom in the hospital. People recovered from ruptured appendices. People didn't die from a little gut incision. Tom was too young. Tom had three kids who loved him with all their hearts. Surely God would be kind and compassionate. What would she do without Tom? The kids and Tom were all that was left to her family.

"I know you're out there, so you might as well come in," Tom called hoarsely.

"How'd you know I was out here?" Annie asked.

"I smelled your perfume."

"I got here as soon as I could. How are you, Tom?"

"My throat is sore from the tube they had down it. My gut hurts. The good news is I'm going to live to walk out of here. For God's sake wipe that awful look off your face, Annie."

"I'm sorry. I was . . . You know, remembering."

"Yeah, I know. I was thinking the same thing myself when I came in. I'm going to be all right, Annie. How's things going?"

"Believe it or not, things are running smoothly. You said you needed to talk to me about something important. Are you up to talking about it now?"

"Mandy brought my briefcase last night. Open it up and spread it out."

"Tom, you are a pack rat. What is all this stuff?"

"Look, kiddo, we have to make some decisions. Time has just galloped by. You opened your first shop in 1980. It's now 1993, thirteen years later. You own eighty-four Daisy Shops. It's time to discuss the franchising of those shops. Every single one of them is profitable to the point of being obscene. You're a multimillionaire. So am I, thanks to your generosity. My kids' futures are secure, again thanks to you. You have one of those old mansions on the battery filled with priceless antiques, you drive a pricey sports car, you set up a trust fund for your godchild. You were named Woman of the Year, three years running. You set up a scholarship fund on every campus where we have shops. You, little sister, have done it all. I guess my question is, how much more money do you need or want. What you have now will last you several lifetimes even if you go decadent on me. God, I forgot the animal shelters you built and fund along with the pediatric wings you've built onto four different hospitals. What's left to do, Annie?"

"The homeless, more food for them, better conditions."

"Annie, we took care of that last year."

"Summer camps for inner-city kids."

"We set that up two years ago. The funding is secure."

"A memorial for Mom and Dad. Something in good taste."

"It's under way, Annie. Sometimes it's hard to give money away."

Annie felt the blood drain from her face. She sat down. "Yes, sometimes it is."

"You look . . . ghostly. What's wrong?"

"I forgot to eat in my haste to get here. I'll grab something in the cafeteria when I leave. You know me, eat, eat, eat."

"So, do we go for it or not?"

"How many do you want to franchise?"

"All but four."

"Which four, Tom?"

"Well, I thought we'd keep the two in Charleston, your first one and Jane's at the Baptist College. I'd like to keep the two here in Clemson. My kids can work summers and holidays. I don't want life made that easy for them. We can handle two. I know you won't want to part with the first one. Check with Jane. She might want to put hers on the block."

"What kind of money are we talking about, Tom? Have you really thought this through?"

"I really have, Annie. Look, it's time you got a life, and I sure would like more time with my kids. Mandy's going off to college next year. But, to answer your question, I thought two hundred fifty thousand dollars was good per store. That would gross twenty-one million. That's not the end of it. You'll get a percentage every year. If the new owner fails, the store reverts back to you. It's more involved than that, but you have the gist of it. Each owner buys from our supplier, they adhere to our promotions. There will be more than enough money coming in to fund all your charitable works. You would, of course, retain the right to open more stores anytime you saw fit. The lawyers have to work that out. Taxes have to be paid, that kind of thing. What do you think?''

''It's going to be difficult to let go of thirteen years of hard work, Tom. What will I do?''

''You're going to take a vacation, and you're going to smell the roses. That's what you're going to do. You've done it all. Kick back before it kicks you.''

''Okay.''

''You're sure, Annie?''

''I'm sure. When do you want to get this under way?''

''When I get out of here. I can make phone calls sitting on the couch with my feet up. I can get it all started. But, and here's the big but. There's a clunker in everything. Since coffee is the main ingredient in this operation, it is of major concern when the price goes up. Take a look at the coffee figures.''

''We use, give or take a few pounds, around twenty pounds of coffee a day. If you multiply that times six it comes to one hundred twenty pounds a week multiplied by twenty-four days a month is two thousand eight hundred eighty pounds a month. Times eighty-four stores it's roughly two hundred forty-two thousand pounds a year. Your old friend gave us a good deal twelve years ago. That deal is no longer working. There's someone new in charge now, Kiki Aellia. Decaf is suddenly off the charts. We have to step up to the plate on that one. I want you to go to Hawaii and work some magic. If the Grayson Coffee Company raises its prices, we're going to have to look elsewhere. That's if we want the franchises to work. I can't go, Annie. I'll be laid up for at least six weeks. This operation was not a piece of cake. We can get things under way, but we need a better coffee deal. Can you do it? No, that's wrong, will you do it?''

Annie sucked in her breath. ''Do you think I could take Rosie and Harry with me?''

''Why not. Buy them seats on the plane. Better yet, charter

a flight and they can have the whole damn plane to romp in. Charge it to the business. This is business of the highest order. Stay as long as you like. Call me, fax me, send up a smoke signal. Whatever. Go swimming, snorkeling, sun yourself, get a gorgeous tan. Go naked dressed in a lei. Do what you want to do, Annie. If you don't want to stay in Hawaii, go somewhere else. You followed your dream, now it's time to live it.''

Annie laughed. "You should have been a used-car salesman, Tom. Okay, okay, I'll do it. When do you want me to leave?''

"As soon as possible.''

"How does the end of the week sound? I need to shop, charter the plane, take the dogs to the vet, get them traveling shots. I'll leave Sunday. Are you sure you're going to be all right with me gone?''

"For God's sake, Annie, of course I am. Talk to the doctor if you don't believe me. Go home now. I'm expecting a visitor.''

"Who?''

"None of your business.''

"Is this a serious lady, Tom? Who is she? What's her name? Do the kids like her?''

"Yes, it's serious. Her name is Lillian and she's a schoolteacher. One of Ben's teachers, in fact. The kids love her, and she loves them.''

"And you didn't tell me! How could you keep something like that from me? I'm your sister!''

"The same way you wouldn't tell me where you got the hundred grand to buy off Mona. Jeez, I'm sorry, Annie. I didn't mean to say that. I know we agreed never to mention it. I didn't tell you because I wasn't sure. You know, if you talk about it, something will go wrong. I didn't want anything to go wrong. When you get back, I'd like to drive down to Charleston and have you meet her. She reminds me of Mom when Mom was young, and we were kids. She kind of smells like her, too.''

Annie leaned over the bed. "I'm glad you found someone,

Tom. Okay, I'm on my way. I'll call you before I leave for any last-minute instructions. Do we set up an appointment or what?"

"Nope, cold turkey. Catch Kiki off guard. They aren't expecting us to complain. Be that hard-nosed businesswoman I know you can be. If you don't like their deal, leave. Don't be afraid to pull out your ace in the hole even if we aren't one hundred percent committed to it. Selling coffee by the pound or half pound in the shops will increase revenues greatly. An additional three to four hundred thousand pounds of coffee a year should make anyone sit up and take notice. We'll start small, and I'll work on the remodeling aspect while I'm home recuperating. Kiki doesn't have to know we aren't set to go on it. I merely alluded to it, and I heard the old salivary glands watering. All the way from Hawaii. If that doesn't work, we'll switch to Plan B. Whatever you decide is okay with me. Let's be clear on that, okay?"

"We're clear. Charter a plane? That's definitely decadent, Tom. I'm gonna do it."

"See you around, kiddo. Don't be afraid to kick some ass. Hey, how's Elmo?"

"Not good, Tom. He's looking at his eightieth birthday. He's got some problems, but we still have dinner together three nights a week. I'd give up the shops before I'd give up those dinners. He never forgets to bring a chewie for Rosie and Harry. I love that old man."

"I know you do, sis. Take care of him. Hey, take him to Hawaii with you. Bet he'd love that."

"That's a great idea. Get better quick, Tom. You'll see me when you see me. Don't forget, we have a date so I can meet Lillian."

"You won't let me forget. Get out of here," Tom groused. "It's almost time for Lillian to get here."

"I'm going, I'm going."

* * *

Annie felt every inch a princess when she trooped up the steps of the private jet that would take her all the way to Hawaii. Rosie, Harry, and Elmo had boarded five minutes earlier. Money was a powerful aphrodisiac, she thought. At the precise moment she stepped into the plane and stewards and pilot welcomed her, she knew she could do anything she wanted to do.

She could even call Parker Grayson or better yet, take a trip up to the North Shore and say, "I was in the neighborhood." Absolutely she could do that. Of course she would do no such thing. *Then why did you buy all those designer clothes and shoes? Liar, liar, pants on fire.*

Annie buckled the two shepherds into their seats. Elmo sat in the middle while she sat across the aisle. She buckled her own seat and smiled at Elmo. "I hate to fly."

"I'm not fond of it myself. The truth is, it's safer than riding in a car. Okay, everyone, here we go! Up up and away," the old man chortled. Harry barked and Rosie joined in. Annie simply gritted her teeth.

Elmo accepted the glass of wine the steward handed him. Annie did likewise. "Please give the dogs some root beer," she said to the steward.

"There are rules. I can't serve dogs." Harry barked sharply at the steward's tone.

"There aren't any rules on this flight. I paid for four passengers. The dogs each have a seat. I explained about the dogs when I chartered this flight. I'd suggest you move your ass and get the root beer. If you don't have root beer, 7UP will do. If you don't, you won't be with us when this flight returns to Charleston. You can find your own way home from Hawaii. Or, you can get off in Dallas when we set down there. It's your call," Annie snapped.

The steward marched off. He returned with two bottles of root beer. "Didn't you forget something? These dogs are talented and incredibly protective but they do not know how to swig out of a bottle." Elmo guffawed until he choked. Harry licked at the tears trickling down the old man's face.

"This is going to be a fun trip." Annie giggled. "I had our lunch catered. You're going to love it, Elmo. Do you think you'll miss your lady friends?"

"Nope. Wouldn't even tell them where we're staying. They'd be calling all hours of the day and night. One of these days they're going to smother me. I love the attention, but sometimes it gets to be too much. Are you gonna be seeing that coffee fellow that broke your heart?"

There was no use in pretending she didn't understand what he was saying. Elmo knew her too well. "No. And he didn't break my heart. There was something off-kilter about him. To this day I can't put my finger on it. I was smitten, though."

"Then why'd you do all that shopping last week. You bought out the stores," Elmo said as he poured root beer into two plastic dishes.

"Because I'm rich, and I can shop till I drop. Everyone wants new clothes when they go on vacation. You didn't say a word when I gave you the new stuff I bought for you."

"That's different. Don't let me forget to bring back two grass skirts. Did you spend a lot of money?" Elmo asked slyly.

"A fortune. More money than I ever spent on clothes in my life. I bought a Chanel handbag, Elmo. Guess how much it cost."

"Two hundred dollars?"

"Try twenty-two hundred dollars."

"Mercy!"

"Before you can ask, I spent seven thousand bucks. I almost got sick when I tallied it up. I went crazy."

"I'd say so. Looks to me like the tranquilizers the vet gave these dogs is kicking in. What should we do?"

"Read. Or, I can have the steward put on a movie. You have to wear earphones to hear the voices. If you plug in the headset, you can hear music. If you move over here, we can play cards. Or we can take a nap."

"Let's just talk. Do you know what I heard on the news last night?"

"News?" Annie giggled.

"Yes, news but Boston news. Remember that kid that went to prison for stealing the money? He's getting out a few years early for good behavior. He's over thirty now. Imagine that. He spent the best years of his life in jail. He said something I really didn't understand. He said if the money had been recovered immediately, he wouldn't have had to serve all that time. Can that be true, Annie?"

"I don't know, Elmo. I didn't watch the news last night. When that insurance investigator was dogging all of us he never said anything like that. Maybe it's something he wants to believe. Robbery is robbery."

"What tickles me to no end is half the money being returned. When it was returned all those years ago, they said it was *fluffy*, like someone washed it in fabric softener."

"Elmo, do you believe everything you hear?"

"In this case I do. They showed the kind of money bag the bonds and money were in. When the person returned it, it filled three big garbage bags. *Fluffy* was what the reporter called it. There wasn't one fingerprint on any of the money, the bonds, or the bags."

"I guess fluffy is better than nothing. They probably found some prints and just aren't saying they did."

"Nope. Not a one. That insurance man said he personally inspected each and every bill and it took him *forever*. The insurance company got half their money back from the bank. Everyone's happy but the kid in jail.''

''You see, Elmo, that's the part that doesn't make sense. He should be happy he's getting out of jail early. I don't want to talk about it. I keep remembering how miserable that man made all of us.''

''It's okay with me, Annie. I didn't mean to upset you. I knew that old fool wouldn't get anywhere harassing us. Are you going to your fifteen-year college reunion later this month?''

''Jane asked me the same thing not too long ago. She wants to go. I've been thinking about it. Fifteen years is a long time, Elmo.''

''When you're my age, it's even longer. I'd like to see the old store again. I liked talking to the kids and hear them call me Pops. Guess it will depend on how I feel at the time. The man that bought my store promised to send me back my sign, but in thirteen years he never did. I called him and wrote a dozen letters. You don't think he's still calling the store the Richardson Pharmacy, do you?''

This was safe ground. ''Could be. I'll have our lawyer look into it. Was it part of the contract?''

''Yes, it was. When I die, I want that sign to go with me. Make a note of that, Annie.''

''Stop talking like that, Elmo. You told me that three hundred times and three hundred times I said okay. You're going to live to a hundred and ten. You know how psychic I am.''

''About as good as I am at predicting rain,'' Elmo snorted. ''I'm going to take a nap.''

Annie stared straight ahead until her eyes started to water. She thought about the strange tone she thought she'd heard in Elmo's voice. Almost as though he was trying to warn her of something. There had been moments over the years when she thought the pharmacist suspected something. But then she'd thought Jane felt the same way. All the while it was Jane Peter

Newman was homing in on. Guilty. Guilty. Guilty. Did people who got out of jail really go after vengeance? Wasn't jail supposed to rehabilitate the prisoner? Would the kid who was no longer a kid throw in his lot with the insurance investigator? To what end?

"Phooey on the lot of you," Annie muttered. "I'm off to Paradise, and I'm not going to think about any of that junk now. Maybe later. A lot later." For now she was going to close her eyes and dream about wearing the rainbow island dress Mattie had made for her years ago. Where she would wear it, she had no clue. She supposed she could wear it to sit behind the waterfall Parker had taken her to. Maybe, if she was lucky, she'd see Annie's Rainbow again. Where are you, Parker? What are you doing right this minute? Do you have a sixth sense that soon I'm going to be within shouting distance? Is there even the remotest possibility that we might run into each other? She wished now that she had called Daniel on some pretext or other and in some offhand way, casually mention that she was going to Hawaii. *Why didn't I do that? Because I'm a fool, that's why.*

A moment later she was sound asleep. She didn't wake until the steward tapped her shoulder lightly. "Fasten your seat belt, Miss Clark, we're about to land."

Annie walked the groggy dogs while Elmo opted to stay on the plane. They were airborne again forty minutes later. She closed her eyes in the hopes she could continue the wonderful dream she was having about Parker Grayson.

It wasn't to be; a dark-eyed young man wielding a gun, a money bag slung over his shoulder, stalked her as she tried to hide behind the waterfall where she'd spent blissful hours with Parker Grayson. Lurking on the other side of the falls was Peter Newman in a yellow-rubber raft, a gleeful expression on his face. "Gotcha!"

Annie woke with perspiration dripping down her face. Elmo

looked at her with worried eyes. "What in the name of God is wrong, Annie?"

"I just had a horrible dream. I guess it's all the excitement," Annie said as she dabbed at her face with a tissue from her purse. "Plus, I didn't eat today. Are you ready for lunch? We could watch a movie while we eat if that's okay with you. I ordered some very good wine to go with lunch."

"Then, let's do it, girl."

"You look pretty darn spiffy, young lady," Elmo said as he walked Annie to the taxi that would take her to the Grayson Coffee Company. "You will charm those Hawaiians right out of their sarongs."

Annie giggled. "They don't wear sarongs here, Elmo. I'm not even sure they wear grass skirts. The women wear colorful island gowns called muu-muus. I have one I can model for you. I'm going to get one to take home to my niece. Are you sure I look okay?"

"You look better than okay. You look like a model in that dress. Tip the hat a little. Didn't know women still wore hats," Elmo grumbled.

"Everyone wears them in the sun. It sure is hot. Don't keep the dogs out too long and make sure they have plenty of water."

"I've been baby-sitting these dogs for years. I guess I know how to take care of them. Still beats me how you got the condo management to agree to dogs," Elmo continued to grumble.

Annie rubbed her thumb and index finger together. "It's called money, Elmo. I'll call you when I'm heading back. We'll go out to dinner, walk around a little if you feel up to it, drink some wine on our terrace, hit the sack, and do some sight-seeing tomorrow. We'll rest up and head for Maui the next day. I think Maui is the prettiest island of them all. See you later."

In the taxi, Annie took great pains to smooth her dress and sit up straight, so she wouldn't be mussed and wrinkled when she showed up on Parker's doorstep. Would he be there? Would he join in the meeting? How would he look? What would he say? She'd rehearsed her responses and initiated others the night before until the wee hours of the morning. She didn't want to think about the possibility of Parker not being in the offices. He'd said he worked long hours, sometimes from five in the morning till ten at night. Who was Kiki Aellia? His assistant? A partner? An executive secretary? She didn't even know if Kiki was a man or woman, not that it mattered. She should have asked Tom for more details.

Annie stretched out her legs. The panty hose had been a mistake, but her legs were so white she felt embarrassed. Sheer Nude at least gave her a hint of color on her legs and gave the sexy, strappy sandals a little zip. The lime green linen dress was perfect for the climate. The pearl daisy pin, a gift from Elmo that first year, was pinned on her shoulder. The lime green ribbon around the band of the delicate straw hat was a perfect match. She looked professional and felt as successful as she looked.

If she'd ever felt inferior to Parker Grayson, that feeling had been wiped away. It had taken her a few years to realize her tirade against the coffee king had a lot to do with her own insecurities and feelings of inferiority as well as the other nebulous feeling that wouldn't leave her. She closed her eyes and thought about all the awards, all the accolades, all the honorary degrees, the ceremonies, and the write-ups that had been bestowed on her these past years. Being awarded Business-woman of the Year was something to be proud of. Animal rights organizations had bestowed four Golden Paw awards on her in the last four years. She had so many golden keys to cities all over the country that she'd lost count. "Well done, Annie Daisy Clark," she murmured under her breath.

"Here we are, miss," the taxi driver said, getting out of the cab to open the door for her. "It will be no problem to wait for you."

Annie shrugged down her dress and took a deep breath as she adjusted the gold-and-leather chain of the Chanel bag on her shoulder. *Please let him be here. Please, please, please.*

She was so beautiful she was almost intimidating. Almost. Annie extended her hand, "And you are . . . ?"

"Kiki Aellia. And of course you are Tom's sister, Annie. Welcome to the Grayson Coffee Company."

"Thank you."

"We have a small dining room we can use to have some coffee and sweet rolls or we can sit in my office. I've carved out thirty minutes from my schedule to see you today."

Gee whiz, a whole thirty minutes. Annie felt herself start to bristle. The hell with the dining room. She continued to bristle when she said, "I can state my business in five minutes. I certainly don't wish to intrude on your busy day. A cola would be a little more refreshing than a cup of coffee. Shall we get on with it?" Annie said in a voice that could have chilled milk.

Kiki Aellia's perfectly sculpted eyebrows shot upward. "Certainly," she said, leading the way to a beautiful office filled with native flowers. It smelled heavenly.

Annie sat down and crossed her legs. She knew the woman across from her was assessing the total cost of her clothing as well as the handbag. *Best money I ever spent in my life,* Annie thought sourly. *Where the hell is Parker?*

"Let's cut to the chase, as they say. I cannot handle an increase in coffee prices. In fact, I came here to ask you in person to shave two dollars a pound from your price."

"That's out of the question, Miss Clark. Labor prices have gone up. Kona coffee is primo. We have no other choice. Unlike the other coffee exporters, we have not raised our prices in seven years," Kiki said flatly. "Unless you want your coffee unroasted."

"If that's your final word, then there's no point in my eating into that thirty minutes you allotted me. I would like to leave you with a thought," Annie said, getting up out of the rattan chair. "If I take my business elsewhere, which I will, that means you have to peddle two hundred forty thousand pounds of coffee somewhere else. Where's the logic to that? I don't know if Tom told you or not, but we're adding something new to the Daisy Shops. We're going to start selling coffees by the pound. If our projections are on target, we would be tripling our order. So you see, the price cut is essential. Are you sure you want to risk losing ten million dollars a year? That's at fourteen dollars a pound. Roasted, of course." Annie looked at her watch. She'd used up eight minutes. She smiled sweetly. "I'm staying at the Whaler. Perhaps you'd like to think about this. I'll give you until five o'clock this afternoon. It was nice meeting you Miss Aellia. Oh, my brother said to say hello. I can see myself out. Cat got your tongue? Mr. Grayson seems to suffer from the same affliction when things get to the squeeze area. By the way, where is he?" Annie asked boldly.

"On Maui. He only comes in two or three times a week or so to check on the laboratory. I didn't know you knew my brother, Miss Clark."

Brother! "We met many years ago." *Kiki was Parker's sister.* If Parker's sister was working at the coffee company that had to mean her tirade twelve years ago had hit home. "Your brother owes me twelve thousand pounds of coffee. Feel free to mention that to him." Annie wasn't sure, but she thought she saw shades of panic in the beautiful dark eyes.

"Perhaps I can rearrange my schedule and we can discuss matters. Negotiations are always . . . interesting."

"Perhaps you shouldn't. Rearrange your schedule I mean. I don't negotiate. Heads of state negotiate. I'm just a lowly

multimillion-dollar company that does business with you.
That's just another way of saying we do it my way, or I take
my marbles and go home.'' Annie looked at her watch. ''Oh,
dear, I've taken up four more minutes of your time. Five
o'clock, Miss Aellia. Not one minute later.''

''You drive a hard bargain, Miss Clark.''

''You see, that's where you're wrong. I don't bargain. Fourteen dollars a pound is a fair price. I pride myself on being fair.
Thirteen would be better, but it's such an unlucky number.''

''I'll need to talk to my brother.''

''Do whatever you feel you have to do, Miss Aellia. My
price is firm, and so is my deadline. One more thing. It's a
small matter, but small matters sometimes influence decisions.
You knew we had an appointment today. A car service here
would not have gone unnoticed. I learned early on that the better
you treat a customer, the better the relationship develops.''

''I'll remember that, Miss Clark.''

''So will I,'' Annie said smoothly.

Annie arrived back at the hotel to mass confusion. Hundreds
of guests as well as employees were milling about chattering
like magpies. She asked a young man holding a surfboard what
was going on.

''Water line ruptured. All the floors are flooded. The management is going to relocate all the guests. At no cost.''

Annie stared at the mass confusion, reminded of another
day, years ago, when she'd been at the wrong place at the
wrong time. Her stomach started to churn. A moment later she
saw two streaks of dark movement. Guests scattered as Rosie
and Harry skidded to a stop, sat back on their haunches, then
barked loudly for attention.

Annie tussled with them for a few minutes. ''You're scaring
these people half to death. Show them what ladies and gentle-